D0190009

THIS WAY TO DEPARTURES

LINDA MANNHEIM

Influx Press
London

Published by Influx Press
49 Green Lanes, London, N16 9BU
www.influxpress.com / @InfluxPress
All rights reserved.
© Linda Mannheim, 2019

First edition 2019.

Printed and bound in Great Britain by Clays Ltd, Elcograf S.p.A.

Paperback ISBN: 978-1-910312-43-8
Ebook ISBN: 978-1-910312-44-5

Editor: Kit Caless
Cover design: Jamie Keenan
Cover photo: Copie157
Proof reader: Momus Editorial

For George

TABLE OF CONTENTS

NOIR

'I'd do anything for you,' Sam told me once, when we were making love.

We were in the apartment we'd just moved to in South Beach, and the late afternoon sun slatted through palm leaves and sparked shards of light onto the sheets. The air conditioner was old and loud, and Sam's video camera lay on the floor, where he had put it just as he was about to leave for class. My editor believed I was on assignment at that moment. Sam's and my courtship was still new, just out of the box. He thought I was beautiful, and I wasn't, so he must have been in love with me.

Pelo malo, my Aunt Julia used to say as she stood over me, offended by the curliness of my hair. *La judía* was the nickname she gave me because of my nose.

Sam would come to kiss me goodbye when he was about to leave, trace the contours of my face with his fingertips, and stay. Sometimes his brazen displays of romance so unnerved me, I'd look sideways for a way out.

'I'd do anything for you,' he told me, staring into my eyes.

'I want you to kill my husband,' I told him. 'He has an insurance policy. We can make it look like an accident and we can be together then.'

We collapsed into each other's arms, laughing.

That was the dialogue that became our running joke, our secret language, the code of our commitment.

'Tonight, darling. We get rid of my husband tonight.'

And Sam would ask, 'Does your husband know you're here?'

Over time I perfected the staccato desperation of a 1940s movie star. We'd continue the exchange in restaurants, at parties, in bars.

Once, an acquaintance overheard and misunderstood.

'Laura's not married,' Sam said. 'We live together. It's a game we play.'

Reputability wasn't our strong spot.

Sam had silky auburn hair that he wore tied back, and was widely known among my friends as the last hippie left in Miami. He had run away to Coconut Grove in 1978, when it was still filled with crash pads and hash parties, before the Grove's downtown turned into a shopping mall. Sam had long since gone back to school and gotten clean, but still managed to evoke a certain shunting of the status quo. I was told when I first met him that he had never been seen in any clothes but t-shirts, shorts, and sandals. He'd had a brief career as a child actor and automatically tried to lighten every situation he walked into, make the producers like him. I appreciated his ability to improvise, his flashing hazel eyes.

When we were at the beach, we walked into the waves until the water made us weightless and Sam could lift me without effort as if I were a newlywed he was carrying away. I put my arms around his neck and told him, 'I feel like I'm in a war movie and this is our last night before you ship out.'

'Darling,' he said, 'I leave for Iwo Jima tomorrow.' And then Sam hummed a mournful disaster-is-coming song while he carried me further into the waves.

We had a stack of movie jokes.

But it was noir that we came back to again and again, noir that we loved – film noir, with its shadows and horizontal lines and slats of light seen through venetian blinds. Film noir, that American post-war phenomenon of doom and danger about how the war might be done and the boys might be home, but nothing would go back to normal. The French named the genre 'black film' for its darkness. Sam's big project at school was a film that mimicked the soul of these stories but brought you a beat away from them, a knowing and updated version of noir.

Everyone's corrupt. Danger and death wait in each vacant room. Lovers betray one another. The femme noir is alluring but chameleon-like; the protagonist can't stay away from her, but will never actually know who she is either. And the story is told entirely in flashback. It starts with the end, the protagonist telling the police what happened, and you, who are watching, know, as the story unfolds, that there is no hope in this situation – everything has already happened and there isn't a damn thing anyone can do about it.

It was November 1, 1986 and 304 people had been murdered
in Miami so far that year. Dominic, whose desk was next to
mine and whose wisdom and resistance to flack I relied on,
had the police beat. He had been told by his editor that he
couldn't cover every murder and shouldn't even try, but he
tried. He was never around anymore. Sometimes I saw him
at night. He'd gotten into the habit of taking a two-hour
break in the evening to drink as much as he could before
going back to work. He'd been an overseas correspondent
in Nicaragua and El Salvador before he'd come back home
to have his marriage fall apart and his best friend turn up
dead – the kind of suicide that came at the end of long, long
lines of cocaine.

I knew the bar where Dominic spent time – it was a
place that none of the other *Record* reporters went. He had
no interest in discussing his day with anyone. Sam and
I were invited with the unspoken provision that we not
ask Dominic what he was writing unless he first raised
the topic.

I worked for the 'Neighborhoods' section of the *Record*
covering Miami Beach. My editor was sure the paper was
going to fold and had begun investing in Beach real estate.
He was somewhat preoccupied with his investments, and
didn't seem to notice that I steadily and grandly lied about
how long it took me to cover a story. The assignments were
supposed to play up the best parts of the gentrification that
was beginning in South Beach. South Beach, back then,

was retirees and Marielitos and cocaine kings; rundown buildings with wire mesh over the windows lined the streets and vacant storefronts pockmarked the paranoia-strewn pedestrian mall on Lincoln Road. My stories were crap, and it took me about a quarter of the time I said it did to produce them; the *Record* always got my first drafts. I was sick of interviewing optimistic community activists and promising high school students. I was waiting for something to happen.

And that was when he walked in.

He had owl eyes so deep and ringed with dark, he looked like bad memories and brutal worries were at the foot of his bed every night. His straight jet hair was just a little too long and slightly mussed, like some glitter era pop star, and his smooth olive skin had recently been under a lot of sun. His face was perfectly symmetrical and proportioned, which would have made him dauntingly handsome, if it weren't for those painfully sad eyes. He had on a shortsleeved button-up shirt made of cotton so thin, I could see the outline of a silver religious medal he wore underneath. His trousers were brown and somewhat worn, but perfectly pressed. I guessed he was about my age – in his mid-twenties – and he walked right up to my desk, saying my name as if it was a question, and putting out his hand to shake mine with a strong, desperate grip.

I wondered how he had gotten past reception. That was the year bungling bank robbers had a shootout with the FBI in Unincorporated Miami-Dade. Cocaine kept the economy going when tourism dropped off. In the

Everglades, Nicaraguan exiles had been training to join the Contras, squatting in the swamps with shiny mortar launchers. Dominic was always coming across something he wasn't supposed to see and received death threats more regularly and convincingly than any of the other reporters. Security in the newsroom was particularly tight that year.

'I'm Miguel Reyes,' the sad-eyed stranger told me in slow Salvadoran Spanish. 'Alida told me to come see you.' His hands grappled for a moment, then settled on a small nylon duffel bag he'd slung over his shoulder, as if he was trying to find something to hang onto. 'Alida Rivera. You grew up together in New York, yes? She told me to come find you in Miami, but when I tried the telephone number she gave me, it didn't work.'

'I moved a couple of months ago,' I told him. Had moved in with Sam, and Alida didn't even know that yet – she and I didn't keep in touch regularly enough for that. 'How do you know Alida?' I asked Miguel.

'I—' he began. He paused and looked around nervously.

'I'm sorry,' I said. 'How rude of me. Please, sit down.'

I have been told, by more than one person, that my personality changes when I am speaking Spanish – that I am more obsequious, more polite. As Miguel sat in the plastic chair beside my desk, I offered him some coffee. He said he couldn't, that he didn't have much time. There were friends of his he needed to find from El Salvador. It was urgent that he get a message to them, but they had become lost, here in the United States, after fleeing his country because of the war. Inez had given him my name, told him that if I wasn't able to help, I would know someone who could. He had first looked for his friends in New York, and had met Inez through New York CISPES – the Committee in Solidarity with the People of El Salvador.

Now he leaned over and unzipped the duffel bag he'd placed on the floor – it was the sort that middle-class men used to carry their gym clothes and less fortunate men used to carry their belongings when they weren't sure where they were going to be staying that night. Quickly, Miguel pulled a battered manila envelope from the bag, but before he zipped it again I caught a glimpse of what was inside – a worn t-shirt, a tattered towel, a little black pouch that probably held his shaving things.

He caught me peeking, looked up, and smiled, then placed the photos on the desk – stilted portraits of a young woman with wavy brown hair, and a young man whose eyes burned with anger. The woman looked as if she had played a joke that the photographer would soon discover, the man as if he wanted the photo session to end quickly because it was a frivolous thing in a world where there was no room for frivolity: as soon as that photo session was over, he was going to go back to seeking justice. Both photos seemed strangely out of date. 'My friend,' Miguel explained, pointing to the man. 'Back when we lived in La Libertad. Esteban Reyes, and his wife, Marisol Jovel.'

They had been gone several months now, he explained, had last phoned from New York to say they were leaving for Miami to start factory jobs, but had not been heard from since.

'Alida thought I could help you?' I asked.

'She said you know people,' he explained, fidgeting again, moving the photos back and forth. 'No conozco Miami. No conozco a nadie por aqui.'

Alida was exactly the sort of person who would land me with a lost exile even though we hadn't seen each other in over a year.

'Esteban's mother isn't well,' he explained. 'She may not live much longer, and I have to find him.'

I watched him for a moment. Something about the situation wasn't right, but I couldn't have said what it was. Alida once said I'd make God show me the Ten Commandments carved in stone before I'd believe them, and I was jealous of the ease with which she welcomed people in trouble. She was always doing something good, meaningful. I was writing articles about art gallery openings and cafes that specialized in fresh fruit smoothies. Maybe I could redeem myself by helping this guy find a friend who needed finding.

'What did they tell you before they left New York?' I asked him.

I drove Miguel to some of the refugee agencies in Little Havana – it was good for him and good for my ego. Introducing myself as a *Record* reporter got us an attentive audience, especially among officials trying to curry favor after some scandal or other. But everyone who saw the photos shook their heads. They'd usher us out of their offices and back into waiting rooms filled with scared mothers and screaming kids, and Miguel and I would climb back into my beat-up Toyota to cruise down Calle Ocho, its low, drab cement buildings slapped with cast-iron burglar bars and brightly colored signs to evoke the world left behind: El Malecón, Yemaya's, La Carreta. Miguel had arrived on the bus from New York the night before, and now he was sharing a room in a Little Havana boarding house with three others – one was a drunk, he told me, forcing good humor as he looked out the window. The man had come into their room roaring with anger at two o'clock in the morning. Another had eyed his duffel bag – he didn't dare leave anything in the room. He took another sip of the café con leche I'd bought him. He told me he was sorry if he wasn't acting like himself.

Miguel, in the passenger seat of my car, started to strike me as the kind of companion I'd been missing in this city of slick cars and fake tans. He put things in perspective by telling me of his trials. His problems were the kind of problems that people had back home; you had nothing and could do nothing, and therefore everything was out of control. Did I think of us going off on some kind of existential road trip? Maybe, a little. Did I think of him like a buddy in a buddy movie joining me to take on a mission that meant one thing to him and another to me? Yes, I did.

Then I came to my senses. He was a complete stranger. A bar-room pronouncement of Dominic's came back to me, his explanation for why men like him became obsessed with the murders they wrote about: *you look for what's lost because you're lost.*

I pulled up in front of the Magic Blanket factory in Hialeah. 'Hay algo que tengo que decirle,' said Miguel, so softly I could barely make out his words. 'Esteban and Marisol were receiving warnings.'

'Warnings?' I repeated.

Miguel's eyes seemed to sink deeper. 'Before they left El Salvador. From La Mano Blanca.'

'The death squad?'

He nodded. 'One morning they came home to find a white handprint on their door.'

La Mano Blanca's warning.

'And that was when they left Salvador,' I concluded.

Miguel nodded. 'They were union organizers,' he explained further.

'And they're not here legally,' I guessed.

There was a pause, as if he was waiting to see what I would do with this information.

I wasn't sure how much Alida had told him about me. By the sounds of it, not much.

'And I received the warning too,' he said.

He had sunk back into the seat, and I was watching him to see if something would reveal that his story was manufactured. But I couldn't find any seams on it, no trademarks, no twitches, no hollows in the center of his voice. He held the coffee cup like it was a talisman, hands trembling slightly, shoulders hunched, eyes directed right into mine – exactly like a man who had revealed a dangerous secret. I remembered the instructions Inez and I had been handed when, as children, we went out to play in the street: strangers should be left as you found them, sob stories promptly returned to their owners. Somewhere along the way, Inez had decided to dismiss this as cynicism rather than wisdom; no one we knew had ever stayed safe by avoiding risk.

'We'll find Esteban,' I said.

By the time I dropped Miguel off at the boarding house, the sun was setting. The manila envelope with the photos inside was sitting on top of a stack of papers in front of the stick shift. The images were more rumpled and stained – I'd been taking them out and handing them to strangers all day long. 'I'll talk to my friend tonight,' I assured Miguel. 'But I need to meet with him alone first.' Miguel nodded, but looked as if he didn't want to leave the car. I was already late to meet Sam and Dominic at the bar, and not about to explain to Miguel that Dominic entertained neither friends nor strangers at the end of his eighteen-hour work days. The death threats meant he liked familiar places and familiar people. There was a limit to the familiar people he spent time with too. He could talk to cops and autopsy technicians, but not to anyone who raised things that were trivial – he couldn't believe the things people complained about, how it was they worried about air conditioning, office politics, traffic.

'Call me tomorrow at the paper,' I told Miguel. 'I'll tell you what I find out.' And then, I put my hand on top of his and squeezed it. He looked at me, eyes softening, and I took my hand away. My face heated.

He opened the car door and stepped out. 'Que Dios la bendiga,' he said, under his breath, before shutting the door.

As he walked toward the boarding house, with all the men outside drinking from bottles in paper bags, his head was bowed and he pulled the duffel to him as if it could offer comfort, almost cradled it in his arms.

The Bull's Eye was the kind of bar that no self-respecting journalist would spend any time in, and was Dominic's favorite place to go. White guys who'd fled to the suburbs parked behind the building surrounded by derelict houses as if it was still their neighborhood bar. They came to the Bull's Eye after a day of delivering beverages, taking tourists out on boats, repairing cars. They picked up big cheap drinks at the bar and carried them over to where the other men chugged their big cheap drinks and played darts. There were dartboards everywhere, some covered with pictures of bad bosses and local politicians and every foot of the rough wood decor was cratered by the sharp points of darts. And among the men playing – they were all men – I found Sam and nearby Dominic, who was about to throw a dart at a dartboard covered with a map. Sam kissed me hello. It was a Bull's Eye tradition to shout at your companions just as they were about to throw. 'You're gonna have to take Sam and me to wherever that lands,' I informed Dominic, who turned around and grinned.

He faced the dartboard and hit dead center, which on the Bull's Eye map was Miami.

Sam and I groaned with disappointment.

'I'm getting more drinks,' Sam announced, waving off Dominic's insistence that he would.

Dominic and I went to a table in the corner and I pulled out my tobacco and started to roll a cigarette. 'Tan pretencioso,' Dominic teased. 'Also, that stuff's going to kill you.'

I licked the gummed end of the rolling paper and smiled. Dominic had the hunched-over stance of an adolescent boy embarrassed by his height. He wore his Levi's big, trying to hide the beginnings of a paunch, and a few years of hard drinking after his wife left him made him look older than he was.

'*I'm* pretentious?' I asked. 'What kind of guy can't even get his dart to land somewhere outside his home town?'

He glanced at the tobacco packet and asked, 'Qué clase de Boricua fuma Drum?'

'I'm Nuyorican,' I answered in English, lighting my cigarette. 'We've already established I'm not authentic.'

I slipped the manila envelope from my bag and put it on the table.

'Doesn't Sam want you to stop smoking?.'

'Sam really loves me,' I informed him. 'It's okay with him if I get cancer.'

Then I took the photos from the envelope, and explained, in Spanish, 'A friend of a friend came to the newsroom today. Anda buscando estos Salvadoreños.''

Dominic looked at the photos and hooted, 'Carajo! Who are they? Least popular in their high school class?' He started to laugh.

'Dominic, please. They're union organizers. They left El Salvador because of death threats. Their friend came to the United States to find them, but they've disappeared.'

Dominic's eyes watered then, just as if someone had punched him hard in the stomach. He drained the dregs from his glass.

Two bodies had been found the week before in a rooming house in Sweetwater – a man and a woman, young. They hadn't been in the rooming house for long, only a few days.

The others knew them only by their first names, Reinaldo and Paula. They spoke Salvadoran Spanish. They said they worked in a factory. There was nothing left in the room to identify the couple past their first names. They'd paid the initial week's rent in cash.

Dominic conveyed this after Sam returned to the table with our drinks. The photos lay on the table like accusations. Dominic slugged down some beer and stared at the images.

'Dominic,' I whispered. 'Is it them?'

'I don't know,' he told us.

Sam looked at me with lowered eyebrows, and I shrugged.

'The bodies were pretty messed up,' Dominic said, looking down.

'What do you mean?' I asked. 'You mean the way they were killed?'

He shook his head. 'They were killed by bullets,' he told us. 'It's what happened afterwards.'

'Hey, nothing's too gruesome for us,' Sam reassured him.

'Someone cut off their faces,' Dominic said.

Sam grabbed my shoulder.

'Someone cut off their hands.'

I covered my eyes.

Dominic said, 'They couldn't get an ID.'

I uncovered my eyes.

The Bull's Eye customers, in their baseball caps and t-shirts, were gesticulating with their beer bottles, laughing at the same jokes they'd heard over and over. They stood before the dartboards and let their artillery go, and the darts flew and their metal points tore into the cork. I imagined I could hear the thuds, though of course with the din and the music I could not. But it was as if I could hear the thud and then silence again. Mostly, in the noise, I kept hearing silence.

Miguel showed up at the paper the next day, brimming with expectation, a different man. He was waiting for me to give him good news, but I couldn't give it to him. And I still couldn't figure out how to break it. Dominic was right – we didn't know who the corpses were.

'Miguel,' I said when he walked in. 'I was waiting for your call. Sit down.'

He shifted in the chair next to my desk, tapping his foot impatiently, grinning.

'I have some news for you,' I began, 'but—'

'I have some news too,' he interrupted. 'It's about Esteban and Marisol.'

I took a breath and pulled back.

'I found someone who's seen them.'

I swallowed.

'What's the matter?' he asked. 'It's good, no? One of the men in the boarding house took me to see his friend in Sweetwater. He said there was a Salvadoran couple there—'

'Miguel,' I said. My throat closed.

'— and the man was named Esteban.'

'When did he last see them?' I asked. My voice came out lower than I meant it to. 'A week ago,' Miguel continued. 'Esteban told him they'd been fired from the factory. They got some guy angry and they were afraid he was going to call immigration. Se treparon en una lancha en camino a Cuba.'

'What?' I asked.

'They got someone to take them to Cuba by boat. A compañero.'

There was no question that Miguel believed all this. And it was certainly plausible. Dominic hadn't known much about the couple in Sweetwater. Even the names didn't match up.

'The boat captain is in Key Largo,' Miguel continued. He showed me a crumpled piece of paper with the name of a captain, and a boat, and the marina where it was docked.

'That's over an hour from here,' I told him. Without a car, it would take him far longer than that to get there. Once he was in Key Largo itself, he'd have to take a taxi out to the marina, and it would be expensive. His English was minimal.

He could go to Key Largo and disappear. This could be another one of those strange stories Dominic and I talked about in the bar. I could lose track of the ending.

'I'll take you there,' I said, gathering a few things and putting them in my shoulder bag – a notepad, some pens, my tobacco.

When we were in the car, about to drive out, I saw that the tragedy had left his eyes, and without it he really was beautiful. There was a beat of silence. We smiled at one another before I started the engine. 'What did you find out?' he asked me suddenly.

I didn't answer.

'Last night,' he reminded me, 'from your friend.'

'Nothing,' I told him, and pulled out onto Biscayne.

Key Largo wanted all the connection it could get to the Humphrey Bogart and Lauren Bacall film, but the last movie they made together was mostly shot on a studio lot in Hollywood, and until it was released, the land we stood on was still called Rock Harbor. Local business owners lobbied to name their town after a fictional hurricane-hit island. You drove through miles and miles of strip malls to get to the Keys, until you broke through the suburban squeeze and the highway skimmed the top of the water. And, if you continued down to the southern tip, you'd be on a ribbon of land no wider than two old Buicks. Then you'd reach a spread of land again, with clapboard houses and dirt roads trailing between the subtropical tangles of saw grass and sea grape.

We asked for directions at more than one gas station, then drove back and forth three times until we saw the turnoff – hidden by palmetto leaves and marked with a sign that read:

'Private Property. Owners and Guests Only. Visitors and Workers Must Have Permission to Enter First.'

Miguel said he'd been told that the captain would arrive by late afternoon, certainly by sunset, and the sky was darkening, but the darkness owed just as much to an oncoming storm as it did to dusk. There were two yachts tied to the pier, three or four lost-looking fishing boats, and a few ratty rowboats flaking paint.

From the lonely wooden pier there was nothing visible but hungry turquoise sea, unsettled islands, mangrove trees, and hovering anhingas, their crooked necks and wings stubborn and solid, as if they had survived being broken and then put back together again.

'It's beautiful,' said Miguel, coming up from behind me. I could feel his breath near my ear, the heat charge of the coming storm. I turned to him, and then the first drops of rain began to fall.

Then we saw the boat – it was called *The Wrong Impression*. There was no one there, no one responded to our calls. But we climbed on, decided to stay there, and huddled on the deck to hide from the rain.

He was from La Libertad, a village by the sea. At first there had been farmland, but then his family lost it, and there was only work at the factory. When he spoke, it was as if he was telling my own grandparents' story, of losing the place you come from, and I found myself telling him how they had lost their land and left Puerto Rico. And we told each other these things on the boat, under a blue canopy strung across the deck, while the waves slapped against the dock and the side of the boat, and the rain beat down. And by then we were sharing a small ledge, trying to keep from getting wet. Sometimes, we brushed one another's hands when we held onto the ledge. And then our hands were next to one another's, and then his fingers covered mine. And finally, he reached for me, and he kissed me, and I whispered, 'I have a boyfriend.' And I kissed him back.

The rain beat down. He stroked my hair. I lit a cigarette for him and one for me also. The lightning flashed and the boat rocked. He told me about growing up with Esteban in La Libertad. I told him about growing up with Alida in New York. Every now and then he'd ask me something about the Nuyorican Spanish I was using and when we tried to work it out between his Spanish and mine, we'd end up laughing and pull each other closer, and then we'd kiss again. I could feel the warmth of his skin through his thin shirt and the damp around us. I could smell the cheap cologne – like the Colonia de Oro my cousin in Puerto Rico wore – and with it Miguel's sweat, and I buried my head in his neck, inhaling. And then I whispered his name for no reason and he took me in his arms again.

It was getting late. He started to tell me a rambling story about trying to unionize in the factory. He kept going over the same ground again and again – threats from the factory owner, and then the soldiers pounding on his door, on Esteban and Marisol's. *Are you hiding guerillas in here? Are you a communist? Are you hiding FMLN?* And the union organizer who came from the capital, always talked as if he had to squeeze in every word before someone shut him up, and waved his arms, and tapped you on the shoulder and told you, *Don't be scared. You're going to win.*

Miguel imitated the union organizer when he said this. He tapped me on the shoulder, the heat of his fingers leaving their mark. 'You can die on your knees or you can die with dignity,' Miguel said then, in his own voice.

The white handprint appeared on the door of the house where the union organizer lodged with a widow and her granddaughter. La Mano Blanca. The sign of the death squad.

I rolled a cigarette, handed it to him. He didn't take it. I lit a match.

They found the bodies the next night, faceless.

I burnt my hand, dropped the cigarette.

'La Mano Blanca – the military – the same thing – took off the faces of the people in the house.'

I blinked, hoping I'd heard him wrong.

'They took off the faces with a knife and hung the faces from branches of a tree. When killing isn't enough, you must find other ways to terrorize people.' I put my hand on his arm, thought I could comfort him. But he was rock hard.

The rain had stopped. There were only birds, the waves slapping against the sides of the boat, small and even again.

'Esteban and Marisol took over from the union organizer,'

Miguel said, his voice growing smaller. 'And then the white handprint appeared on their door. So they went to the capital. But La Mano Blanca found them there too.'

'So they came to the States,' I finished.

'We had to find them new identities to get them out of the country. Marisol became Paula and Esteban became Reinaldo. We joked that his new name would be Ronald Reagan.'

I shut my eyes.

Miguel took my hand then, as if comforting me.

I opened my eyes.

'There's something I have to tell you,' I said. 'My friend,' I began. It was so dark by then, I could barely see his face. I hesitated, forced myself to keep going. 'My friend who I talked to yesterday—'

I was waiting for Miguel to signal that I should continue, but all he did was drop my hand. He moved away from me a little, squatted down, balanced on the balls of his feet. His elbows rested on his knees, he brought his hands together as if in prayer.

'My friend works the police beat,' I said. 'And he knows there was a couple found last week. They were Salvadoran, and their names were Reinaldo and Paula.'

'It's not them,' said Miguel quickly.

'Someone cut their faces off,' I whispered.

'It's not them,' he said again.

And then, there was a long stretch of silence. A wave bigger than the others slapped the boat and jostled us slightly. I had my back against the galley entrance, but Miguel was caught off balance and I could hear his sneakers skittering slightly as he tried to regain his position. I reached out and grabbed his hand. He dropped it as soon as he stabilized. There was more silence.

'The captain's not coming,' I said finally. 'I'm taking you back to the city.'

Dominic wasn't at the Bull's Eye when we got there. From the pay phone, I could see Miguel standing and waiting, looking lost while the big white guys with their beards and baseball caps barked jokes and brought up their beer bottles. I watched Miguel's eyes darken and flatten, while I said into an answering machine: 'It's Laura. I'm at the Bull's Eye trying to find you. If you—'

A click and then Dominic picked up. 'I'm not required to be there every night.'

'Yes you are,' I said. I twisted around and cupped the receiver with my hand, so the guy coming out of the men's room, hiking up his pants, wouldn't overhear me. 'I'm here with a friend who needs to talk to you.'

A beat of silence. 'Do you want me to give him bad news?'

'Unless you've got some other kind.'

'Bad news is all I've got,' said Dominic. He had a habit of talking too loud on the phone, a habit begun by making calls over the newsroom din. 'I'll be there in a half hour.'

'Dominic,' I said. 'Wait … I … Can we come there? It might be nice to have a little privacy.'

'To my house?' Dominic asked, as if I had suggested we meet that evening in Bolivia.

'Sam's home tonight,' I told him, explaining why my place was out.

Another beat of silence. 'I'm not entertaining much these days.' Then, 'I guess it's okay. This isn't one of the guys who's been making death threats, is it?'

I smiled. Dominic's refusal to ever acknowledge his fears directly, his soft serve comic macho, was one of the things I found so endearing about him. 'He was *getting* death threats,' I answered, agreeing to play the game.

'What?' Dominic asked, as if he'd momentarily been distracted.

'He was getting death threats,' I said again. 'Before he left El Salvador.'

'Oh,' said Dominic. 'Then we have something in common. Bring him over.'

Dominic dwarfed Miguel in every way – when he stood in the dining room, with its dusty cut glass chandelier and its piles of paper on every surface, Miguel looked up at him like a prisoner who could show annoyance with a glance, but not take any action. Miguel's tentative, careful, polite questions were run over by Dominic's skipping Havana Spanish.

Dominic's humor dropped down like rocks on Miguel's mood.

'What's a Salvadoran like you doing in Miami?' Dominic asked, when he returned from the kitchen with another beer. 'All the good guys from your country go to

Los Angeles and Washington.' Dominic sat backwards on a chair, took a long pull at his beer, and put his arms around the backrest as he continued. 'All that's here are the bad guys. The rich sons of whores who fund the death squads. Don't you know that?'

Miguel stared at him.

'Miguel came here to find his friends,' I offered softly.

'You can try to identify the bodies,' Dominic told him. 'But I wouldn't advise contacting the police if you're undocumented.'

There was a long pause in conversation, during which the only sound was Dominic swallowing the rest of his beer.

'Is there something you can tell … you can tell us to help identify the bodies?' I asked Miguel.

'This is nuts,' Dominic announced, to no one in particular.

'No,' Miguel whispered, grabbing at his sleeves.

'I have to get back to work,' Dominic said, rising.

'We can talk about this tomorrow,' I whispered to Miguel.

I rose too. So did Miguel. Dominic walked us to the door and, as he opened it, I told Miguel, 'Go ahead. I'll be out in a minute.'

Dominic was standing against the screen door, on his battered and peeling porch, and I watched Miguel slip into darkness toward the car. I waited until he was out of earshot, then asked Dominic, 'Why were you so hard on him?'

'What are you doing with him?' Dominic countered.

I looked away, fumbled for my car keys.

'Sam really loves me,' Dominic mimicked. 'It's okay with him if I sleep around.'

'What?' I asked.

'Anyone can see the way you look at him,' Dominic said.

'I—' I began.

'Save it,' Dominic told me. He reeked of beer. 'That guy's out of his league. His friends are lying in drawers in the county morgue. And you can't help him.'

'Thanks for everything,' I said, and turned to go.

Miguel was leaning against the car, waiting.

'Perez!' Dominic shouted, when I was halfway down the driveway.

The crunch of gravel as he followed me. Then, softly, in English he said, 'My friends all covered for me when I was cheating on my wife.'

He paused for a minute to take another sip of his beer.

'I just want you to know,' he said, 'If Sam ever wonders where you are, I'm not providing any alibis.'

'Thank you,' I said, turning to go again.

'I'm just telling you,' he called after me.

The storm started on the way to Little Havana; lightning flashed Calle Ocho into black and white relief and the beat of belting rain, of windshield wipers, filled the silence. Miguel put his hand on my leg when the thunder came. I should have pushed it away, but I didn't. On the street, women holding plastic shopping bags over their heads ran for the shelter of shop awnings, huddled in front of darkened storefronts, old men stood in rectangles of light before the still open bodegas. I drove down 14th Avenue and into the parking lot in front of the boarding house. Miguel turned to me. His eyes were bruises. 'I'm sorry,' I said, resigned to the fact that, the way things were playing out, I wouldn't be able to do right by anyone. 'Think about what you want to do,' I told him, taking his hand. 'I'll help you with it. Whatever it is.'

'Will I see you tomorrow?' he asked.

'Yes,' I promised.

He kissed me then, strong and deep, his body arching over the stick shift.

'I'll come for you tomorrow,' I promised.

He opened the Toyota door and ran into the rain, away from me, and I sat in the car for a moment in front of the darkened house. The car felt colder already, empty without him in the passenger seat.

A video tape, and on the video tape scratchy gray figures – a woman with a heartshaped face, a man too adolescent to embody the smoothness he tries to portray. This was Sam's footage for his final project. He was shooting it in Key Largo, in a diner off hours and an empty house nearby and on a back road. And, sometimes, when I came home, he'd be watching that day's footage, on the old TV in our living room, hitting the buttons on the VCR and rewinding it, playing it over and over again.

The woman was telling the man, 'My husband will find out.'

The man was telling the woman, 'I think of you all the time. I can't live without you.'

Student actors, stilted, awkward.

I stood in the doorway, dripping.

Sam turned to me, got up, smile of delight for my arrival, kiss for me. 'Hi, baby. God, you're soaking wet.' He left the room, bare feet thunking against the wood floor, returned with a towel. He dropped it over my head, ruffled my hair with it, dabbed at my face. The towel smelled like him. I took it and let it drop.

'Are you okay?' he asked.

His mussed red hair like a halo, his wrinkled, baggy shorts, his thick cotton t-shirt. I stammered an answer. I was with Alida's friend, all day. We were trying to find some people from El Salvador. We couldn't find them.

Sam's face folded in bewilderment. He swallowed. 'Come on, baby. Speak English to me.'

Had I been speaking Spanish?

The thunder cracked down.

'What about my husband?' the woman on the video tape screamed. The room was dim. The blue of the television bleated against the walls.

I walked into the bathroom, peeled off my clothes, stepped into the shower.

The morning was still inked in darkness when I woke up. Sam was asleep, big and peaceful underneath the sheet, his breathing barely discernible beneath the drone of the air conditioner. I got up, felt for my bag, walked into the kitchen, turned on the light, sat in one of the torn vinyl chairs by the Formica table. Once my eyes had adjusted, I pulled out my tobacco, rolled a cigarette, lit it, exhaled. Footsteps. The door opened. Sam appeared, squinting and naked. 'Sorry,' I said, turning, 'for waking you.'

He acclimated to the light, opened his eyes further. 'You okay, baby?'

'Yeah,' I said. Then, 'I dreamt I was faceless.'

'Anonymous?' he teased with a smile. 'You?'

'No,' I said, taking another drag of my cigarette. 'Faceless.'

He came to me and put his hand under my chin. 'You do not just have a face,' he told me, in a fake Italian accent, 'you have a face so magnificent, every other face on earth should be compared to yours. A man would have to be blind not to see your face.'

I laughed. 'Say that again,' I commanded.

'A man,' he began, in his normal voice.

'No, with the accent.'

'A man would have to be blind not to see your face.'

I took his hand. He stroked my hair. Sam, splatting Hollywood everywhere and making all the bad dreams go away.

I could never tell him everything.

Dominic was on the phone when I walked into the newsroom, standing at his desk and taking the plastic top off a styrofoam coffee cup as he talked, managing to drip coffee on his wrinkled white shirt – he could ruin clothing faster than anyone I knew. His beige chinos had pen marks on them, were big around the waist and gathered with a belt, as if it would be distasteful for him to show he had an ass. He lifted his head in greeting when I got to my desk, looking at me dead on as he practically shouted into the receiver, 'Uh huh. Uh huh. I understand.' He rolled his eyes then and started to smile. I watched, lowering my brows for him to send me a signal about what was happening, but the phone call kept going on, interminable. 'We'd never do that,' Dominic was saying. 'Not in a million years.' Then, 'Uh huh. I understand.'

On my desk was that day's paper, lying flat out so I could read the headline on the front page: 'Suspect in Death Squad Slayings Captured at Dade Home.'

A former Salvadoran army captain described as a major suspect in the 1981 slaying of a US citizen and two Salvadoran clergy members was arrested late Wednesday at his Southwest Dade home.

It looked like a nice story. Bad guy captured and soon to be extradited to El Salvador, eventual justice, someone who was higher up than the low-down henchmen who usually got fingered for death squad killings in Salvador. A stickler would point out the arrest was just a drop in the bucket and the orders to kill came from higher up than this guy. A killjoy would point out that this guy had entered the US two years ago under his real name, stayed the whole time on a tourist visa, bought himself a condo with cash, and swung into the Winn Dixie every couple of days for beer and batter-fried shrimp without anyone noticing until just now. A cynic would wonder what had shifted to end his South Florida holiday.

'You read it through?' Dominic asked, when he got off the phone.

'Yeah,' I said.

Dominic's fingertips touched the edge of his desk. His eyes were burning. 'Good,' he told me. 'Get your little friend out of Florida.'

'Why?' I asked.

'You know where La Mano Blanca comes from?'

'From ORDEN – the paramilitaries.'

'They were trained by the CIA. They get their arms from here.'

'I know that,' I reassured him. I almost rolled my eyes.

'Chickens are coming home to roost now. Your lost cause is going to end up like his friends. Get him out.'

I stared at Dominic, still and silent now but wound tight, like a jack-in-the-box about to slam open its metal lid.

'How do you know this?' I asked.

'I can't tell you. I'm meeting someone tonight. It's all I need for my story.'

Dominic's assessments of danger had never been wrong. He repeated, 'Get your friend out. Now.'

The boarding house was the kind of place where my presence attracted more attention than I was prepared for – men sunk into a beat-up couch in the lobby looking at me with amusement, wondering if I was a just-out-of-school social worker, and, *What do you want here, honey? Something we can help you with?* A big, tired woman behind the counter, color washed out from her hair and the rest of her – her skin, her clothes faded in every way – stood slowly, watching me. She took something out of a drawer, slipped it into a bag next to her, and sat back down like she was wearing weights. 'Miguel Reyes? No, he's gone.' One palm glided against the other to signal departure. 'He left.'

Panic rising, my eyes dampening. She saw and realized I wasn't there on business then.

'Okay, there's a coffee shop down on the corner. Flamingo.' She emphasized the word *Flamingo*, as if I might not get it because of my funny-sounding Spanish. 'He might be there.'

'Thank you,' I called out, as I rushed for the door.

'Okay, mami!'

There was a crowd of men just outside the run-down storefront, waiting to be handed their thimble-sized cups of coffee through the cast-iron grate on the window. A whispered comment from one of the men as I passed – only *Good morning, honey*, but he said it with a breathiness and focus that made it sound like he'd just asked whether I wanted to fuck. On the window someone had painted a big pink flamingo, slightly ill-looking, partially rubbed off. Miguel was behind it, sitting at the counter, sipping his coffee, looking so young and mild that I wanted to put my arms around him and lead him from there, out of the city, to someplace good and safe.

'Laura,' he said, face lighting when I walked in.

I leaned over and kissed him on the lips, sat next to

him on a stool. He took my hand proprietarily. Two young lovers, not yet married, before life wears you down and you avoid one another because you remind one another of your failures. Love, before it's gone bad, gone past its sell-by date. The man behind the counter smiled at its recognition and asked me what I wanted. Miguel and I clutched each other's hands, smoothed each other's clothing, basking in the kind greetings of everyone around us, not a single stranger able to register what Miguel and I knew about and only I knew in detail – the man back home, deceived.

I was going to take him to Key Largo. I was going to find that captain to take him out of the country, or find someone else who could accomplish the same task, but I couldn't somehow. Every now and then you get a moment when a man does exactly what you wish he would: he takes your hand when you want him to take your hand, he decides to leave and come with you when you want him to come along, he leans over and kisses you the first moment you're alone, and you don't have to say anything to make this happen. He just does it, and whatever it is that allows this to happen is as thin as a dragonfly's wing and as big as the sky, and you're not gonna say one word because you don't want to break what makes this happen.

He was in the passenger seat and I was driving us out of the city, staying off the highway, down Old Cutler Road to Card Sound Road, the saw grass and dust edging the asphalt, and every now and then, a barely visible side road, overgrown, that would lead maybe to a lime quarry, or maybe just to beaten swamp and then the ocean again. I reached up and touched his face; he took my hand. I turned off down a side road, held my breath as the Toyota navigated a rut. I had been here before with Sam, when we were scouting locations for the film. We'd driven randomly down the turnoffs until we'd found this one, which opened onto an abandoned quarry. It was a good mile from the road, down ruts and mud, land punished by heat and heavy machinery, brambles and tall grass tangled like razor wire, stretches of barren sand, and beyond that, a rectangle as big as a field scooped of sand and filled with water, the blue and cool of it, as if someone had decided to build an impressive pool here and the mansion would be coming next, and beyond that, more distressed land, and then, the turquoise of the ocean. In Sam's film, under the cover of night, this is where the couple dump the body.

The car doors opened, slammed shut, the only sound there was. I stood near the car, waiting, and he came to me. I put my arms around him, kissed him. He lifted me onto the hood of the car, still hot from the just-stopped engine. I unbuttoned his shirt, ran my fingers along his hairless skin, his prominent ribs. Now, for the first time, I saw the medal he wore under his shirt. St. Christopher, the patron saint of travel. I put my lips to the warmth of Miguel's chest, then brought my mouth to his mouth, slipped my legs around his waist. And if I tell you he was a gentle and solicitous lover, waiting to see how I responded to what he did, whispering my name as he intuitively took away all the fear and ugliness of the world, what will you believe about him when I am done with this story? If I tell you that he wept and that I didn't want to let him go, who will you believe he is?

We heard a noise, unplaceable at first, like an engine. He backed away from me. I dropped to the ground and pulled my underwear on, my skirt down. A car coming. I was sure it would be Sam. Then the hulking sound of an engine pulling something heavy. My pounding heart. I buttoned my shirt. I caught a glance of Miguel, of the fear in his eyes, and in that moment, thought I would kill anyone who tried to touch him. We got into the car. A truck appeared then, beat up and enormous. A voice from high in the cab directed down to us.

'Can I help you kids?'

'No,' I called up, starting the car engine.

'This is private property, you know.' Beard, baseball cap, and late middle age.

'I'm sorry,' I said back, my voice tentative and higher than it ever is, my good girl voice.

Then, looking down at us, the state we were in, it registered – he knew what we'd been up to, averted his gaze. 'Don't stay here too long,' he called out.

He pulled away.

I shut the car off. We watched the truck, slow, lumbering, disappearing down the road.

Miguel started smoothing my hair, pushing some curls to the side while he looked in my eyes. 'It sounds crazy,' he said. 'I was afraid that was your boyfriend.'

I had betrayed, was betraying, Sam in a dozen ways. 'I'm taking you to Key Largo,' I told Miguel.

Miguel stopped stroking my hair, eyes growing larger, sadder. I moved away from him and started the car. 'We can't waste time,' I said.

'What do you mean?'

'I want to find that captain who can get you out of the United States. Enrique Bolando Huerta was arrested yesterday.'

'The army captain,' Miguel said, under his breath.

'He's been living in Miami for two years.'

'What does one have to do with the other?' he asked, looking through the windshield at the water-filled rectangle.

'I don't know,' I admitted. 'But you've got to get out of Miami. I was warned.'

Miguel turned to me, accusation in his eyes. 'You were warned?'

'By Dominic.'

'Dominic!' Miguel snapped.

'He's doing a story on the paramilitaries. He thinks some are carrying out assassinations here.'

'That's not true.'

'It is true. He's meeting with someone later who knows about Huerta.'

Miguel shifted, looking away again. 'Who is he meeting with?'

'I don't know,' I told him. 'It's not important. He was sure about this. He said you have to get out of town.'

'When is this meeting?'

'I don't know,' I told him. 'This afternoon.'

Miguel reached in back then to get his duffel bag. He put it in his lap, unzipped it, and felt for something. Then there was the sound of another zipper, as if he was undoing a pouch.

I thought he was going to show me something. He did. It was a gun.

'What are you doing with that?' I asked.

He shifted and the duffel fell to the floor. He was holding the gun with two hands, one hand high on the drip, other hand around the finger guard. That's when I realized he wasn't showing me the gun. He was pointing it at me.

'Get out of the car,' he said.

He wasn't in the least bit fierce when he said it; he was almost calm, until his words caught in his throat. His eyes were filmed with apology, and his shoulders were pulled in, as if he was repeating a gesture he was weary of. His hands were steady though. The gun was black, big, heavy-looking. I listened for a click – the safety releasing – but there was none.

'You're going to shoot me?' I asked. I had meant it to sound tough, imperious, but the words garbled, dropped, crashed.

His thumb moved against the side of the gun. The safety. No click. Barely a whisper.

'Get out of the car,' he said again. He reached past me, unlatching the door, then shoved me out. I staggered to my feet, breath coming out in millimeters. Then the car door slammed shut and he slipped into the driver's seat. He backed up, terrifically fast, swerved to go down the road, the car flying over the ruts.

I watched for a minute, then ran after him, stumbling on the uneven ground.

Suddenly, the car came backwards. I jumped from its path. He pulled the car near me, and looked out. I waited for him to say something, but he didn't. He threw something out the window. It hit my calf and dropped to the ground. On the ground was a glint of silver. I picked it up. The St. Christopher medal, its chain torn.

I looked up.

'I'm sorry,' he said softly.

He lifted the gun. His fingers met around the grip as if he was praying and I heard the boom as he pulled the trigger.

And then – there is no way to describe this but cliché – the slow motion of it and my paralysis, my heart stopping as he discharged the bullet, the hours that it took for the bullet to leave the barrel and reach my leg, my leg dropping out from under me and the ground suddenly against my chest, the dust rising as I looked up, each speck of it slowly dancing in a brown cloud, expanding and twisting through the air, and the howl I let out as I tried to pull myself up, kept dropping, the sound of traffic I imagined hearing, even though I knew I was too far from the main road to hear anything. Miguel was speeding back to the city, and I was sitting there useless, the red of the pain rising, and the blood from the bullet wound seeping into the soil.

When I regained consciousness and was attended to in the hospital, Sam was there, steady as always. He stayed with me until I could walk again, cooking dinner for us, finding us videos to watch while we huddled together in bed. There wasn't much to say anymore. By then, both of us knew things between us weren't going to last.

I was a very lucky girl, the doctor told me when I took my first steps with a cane. If the bullet had hit the main artery going down my leg, I'd be dead. The near miss was a matter of chance, he said.

Or it wasn't chance, and I'd been shot by someone with extraordinarily good aim, someone well trained.

Dominic had been a no-show for his meeting that day. His body was found on the floor of his living room. The cause of death was a gunshot wound, a single blast to his head.

His face had been removed, his hands cut off.

The bullet found near my leg matched the bullet found near Dominic – military ball ammo fired from a Browning Hi-Power, which was standard issue for CIA agents working in Central America in those days. Since the police discovered this, there have been no new leads.

My car was somewhere on the bottom of a canal, the police guessed. I told them almost everything I have told you. Miami finished the year with a homicide rate of 392. And all this happened a long time ago and there is nothing I can do about it now.

When the girl disappears, no one notices at first. It is fifteen months before anyone contacts the police.

Many things were happening in the city during that time. Buildings were knocked down and there were scandals in the local government. The chief of the big gleaming seaport was found to be taking payoffs and the mayor was accused of hitting his wife. A rental property owned by one of the commissioners was declared unfit for human habitation. Construction finally began on the arts center in the heart of the gutted downtown. In the weedy lots behind the chain-linked fence, near the cement-walled building where skinny men gathered to get their methadone, the city was supposed to be in turnaround.

Just one train line runs through this town, north to south, with stations beyond the best business areas and benches unprotected

from the beat of tropical sun. Children run to the front of the
train so they can look out the window and pretend that it's an
amusement park ride. The reporter, whose car has broken down
again, watches them, thinking about the missing girl.

The last time the foster mother saw the girl was the January
before last. The foster mother told the reporter: *A woman
came to the door of the house. She looked very proper; she was
very well-dressed. She said she was from the Department of
Children and Families, and that the little girl was supposed to
come with her to get some kind of test done.* The foster mother
said she packed up some things – three dresses of the
girl's, a nightgown, a small stuffed bear. She put them all
in one of those little canvas bags that they give to children
who are in the custody of the state. She said the little girl
kissed her goodbye. And then, said the foster mother, the
well-dressed woman took the little girl's hand and walked
down the driveway to a waiting car.

The newspapers are carrying pictures of the girl. They all
carry the same picture: one taken in a shopping mall when
she was three years old. In the photo, the girl's dark face
seems burnished with light. Her large eyes glisten. Her hair
is tied into three braids, each one clasped with a plastic-
beaded rubber band. She is not smiling, but neither does she
look grim. Round-faced as she is, baby chubby, she gives the
impression of an older girl resigned to waiting – waiting to
become a grownup.

This is how the Department of Children and Families found out the girl was missing: a caseworker was fired for falsifying records. A new caseworker was assigned to the girl's case. When the new caseworker went to the girl's foster home, she discovered that no caseworker had visited for eighteen months. *You have custody of the girl,* the girl's foster mother insisted. *Someone from your office came and took her away.*

An email goes out to all the workers in the Department: *Please check all files immediately to see if there is any documentation of the child. This is an urgent matter.*

The supervisor contacts the Department Administrator, who contacts the State Secretary of the Department.

One, two, three, four, five, six days go by. The Department Administrator contacts the head of the county's police department. The police department contacts the newspaper. The newspaper publishes her photograph. The headline reads: *Missing Girl, 5, Gone Fifteen Months.*

They have found a girl's body in another city, in another part of the country. The body they have found is the same age as the missing girl, the same height, the same weight. The body has been found in two pieces, in two trash bags – the arms and legs and torso in one bag, the head in another.

The people in this other city have held memorial services for the girl who was found. They have named the girl Precious. They have said they are all her family.

The authorities test the dead girl's DNA; she is not the missing girl.

We really wanted closure, says a councilman in this city in another part of the country. *But now it's just moving forward and thinking about the other baby. What's her situation? Is she alive?*

The trail is cold, say the detectives. *Very cold.* If they had started the investigation soon after the girl went missing, they might have more to go on. But, now, it is fifteen months later. There isn't much left for them to investigate.

The Secretary of the Department says that she will take full responsibility for the girl's disappearance. The buck stops with her. But, she also wants the newspapers to note that the problem does not appear systemic. The disappearance of the little girl went undiscovered for so long because a caseworker wasn't doing her job. And that caseworker's supervisor. And both have been fired now.

The newspaper carries stories of other children who have disappeared while under the custody of the Department of Children and Families. Four hundred and seven of them missing. *Where do these children go?* asks the article. *How are they misplaced?*

Some of them run away, a judge says to the reporter. *They are placed in foster homes where there are mistreated. They are placed in foster homes that are overcrowded. These children get*

brought into my courtroom, and I tell them: My hands are empty.
I have nothing for you.

The foster mother tells a reporter she called the caseworker again and again and asked when the little girl was coming back. The foster mother says the caseworker always put her off. The foster mother says she was told to keep cashing the little girl's assistance cheques. The foster mother says the caseworker told her, *If we stop those payments, it will take forever to get them started again.*

A couple are watching TV in a city in the middle of the state, far from where the little girl went missing. They take in foster children all the time. There is very little work in this city – its biggest employer is a theme park.

This is the work available here: You can clean rooms in motels that have happy cartoon pictures on the walls. You can weave past queues of families waiting to get on rides and empty garbage cans stuffed with soiled Pampers. You can put grilled hot dogs into pillowy buns while fathers in baseball caps get angry about how expensive everything is.

But instead, the couple take in foster children. One, two, three children sit with them while they watch TV. Four, five, six other children are out playing in the yard.

A picture of the missing girl flashes on the TV. The woman thinks of the little girl who was brought to them the year before – found by the police in a motel room, no identification, barely talking at first.

She looks out the window and sees the girl in the backyard, playing with the other children, waiting to go up the little slide. She watches, and her heart pounds. The girl looks like the one on TV, is the right age, the right height.

The girl's foster mother has a troubled past, the newspapers report. She has been arrested many times, for food stamp fraud, kiting checks, grand theft. She served time in prison once, in another state. She has used many different names during the course of her life. She has been sued by creditors a dozen times. She has sued others. She sued a bus company after she was injured in an accident. She claims that she was never the same afterwards. She claims that she lost her memory.

A couple in a small town have the girl's sister, in another part of the state. She is older, seven years old. People stop the couple sometimes, and say, *That girl looks like the missing little girl.*

The couple knew the missing girl's mother before the missing girl was born. She was a parishioner in their church. She had just one baby then, also a little girl. She couldn't take care of the baby though, on the pipe. *Take her*, she told the couple. And they did, dressed her up for church, combed out her hair. The girl they've raised doesn't know this. She doesn't know she ever had any parents but the ones she's grown up with. The couple have been trying to adopt the girl they've raised for two years, but their calls to the Department of Children and Families went unanswered.

Now, since the story of the missing girl has gone out in the news, the couple have gotten a response. The adoption papers arrive for the girls they've raised.

The detective tells the reporter: *We're still waiting to get the DNA results. I have nothing new for you. I'm sorry.*

He means the results that are supposed to come from the girl placed with the foster family in the city with a theme park.

He suggests to the reporter: *We have many unsolved cases. Perhaps now would be a good time to remind people of that. I have a list of child homicides.*

There was the baby found in the steel bin at the bottom of the trash chute in the condo.

There was the toddler whose body had been dug up from the yard of the family in the working-class suburb.

There is the newborn found in a vinyl gym bag with formula and diapers. She'd suffocated. There was a note with her that said in Spanish: *Please take care of this baby. I cannot keep her. She is the product of a rape.*

The train goes north. The train goes south.

A group of children run to the window that looks out ahead of the very first car and shove one another out of the way, watching the track disappear beneath the train.

The reporter watches.

The missing girl's foster mother explains how she became the missing girl's foster mother: her sister was supposed to become the girl's foster mother. Her sister was friends with the little girl's mother. But when they got to court, her sister realized she didn't have any identification with her.

Since the foster mother had her driver's license with her, she filled out all the paperwork and became the foster mother instead.

The Secretary of the Department for Children and Families is named as a defendant in a lawsuit. Her ex-husband is suing her for charging $10,000 on a credit card in his name.

I didn't want to do this, the ex-husband says, *but this is embarrassing to me. It's ruined my credit rating. I just want her to pay it off. We agreed neither of us would do something like this when we divorced.*

This is a personal matter, the Secretary of the Department tells the reporter.

The child advocate appears before the Blue Ribbon Panel.

Though I address all of you with respect, she says, *I want you to understand how many times I have appeared before panels like this. I want you to understand that when a child dies while under the supervision of the state, and that death receives a great deal of publicity, panels like this come together with the best of intentions.*

She looks down at her papers, adjusts her glasses, folds her hands and looks up again.

Every time, the panels have come to the same conclusions – that we must invest more in the programs. And every time, the state has said that it cannot provide that funding.

The reporter pulls up a story filed three years before, just after the Secretary of the Department was first appointed. *I'm a realist,* she states in the article. *Children are going to die. It's tragic. But this department can't prevent that.*

The presidential hopeful appears at a rally. *We have come together to show that all of us support a little girl who got lost in the world,* he drawls. *We will do everything in our power to find out where she is. But we have, sadly, learned from this that government is no substitute for a strong family.* He glances at his notes. *This is a problem that we cannot solve with money. This is a problem that can only be solved by families. Let me say that one more time: children need strong families.*

The missing girl is spotted in Houston. She is spotted in Cincinnati. She is spotted in Newark, New Jersey. In Nassau in the Bahamas. In Haiti in Port au Prince.

The city grows, changes. Its abandoned downtown is colonized by artists and art dealers. The financial district becomes known internationally. Skyscrapers rise above the harbor.

Almost fifteen years after the girl first went missing, the governor of the state is interviewed. The Department of Children and Families has a new acting secretary.

The governor is asked about the children who have died under the Department's watch over the past six years, the 477 children killed by their parents or guardians. He is asked about the reduction of funding for the Department.

The governor says, *I'm a dad with two girls and three grandsons. Your heart goes out to anybody who's abused or harmed. You want that to happen to nobody.*

A wrecking ball swings against the wall of an old municipal building, knocks it into cement blocks, which drop and knock steel rods twisted in the air. The blue sky beats color through the dust. Traffic whizzes ahead below.

BUTTERFLY MCQUEEN ON BROADWAY

My brother and I go down to Alex's health food store on Broadway. It's the first health food store in Washington Heights. There's a rope of bells that jingles when you open the door. Inside, it looks bare, with wood shelves holding canisters of soy protein, sacks of brown rice, jars of peanut butter.

I am twelve years old, and my brother is twenty-two, and we go in almost every day and talk to Alex.

Alex offers us paper cups of carrot juice. The first time he explains to me how you can get juice out of a carrot, shows me that you drop the carrots into the juicer, pushes them against the blades with a metal plug. The machine whirs. Brightly colored juice falls into a cup. Alex hands it to me and I accept it with suspicion.

It is 1975.

The health food stores – they're all downtown. People who buy their food in these places are called *health food nuts*.

One day, we walk in, and I hear a voice – helium high and sing-song. A little girl, cajoling: 'Alex, why don't you come back to Harlem? We're good to you there.'

But all I can see is an old lady – tiny, in a long flowing skirt, her gray-flecked hair peeking out from an old-fashioned kerchief.

Alex shrugs the question off. Silence, and then a smile, and then: no he won't be coming back. Not after what happened.

The old lady alarms me. How does she know Alex? Why is she trying to get him to move away? And why is she speaking like a little girl?

She puts her packages into a shopping cart, turns to go, and opens the door. The rope of bells play. And then she's gone.

My brother, astonished, asks Alex, 'Was that Butterfly McQueen?'

'That's Butterfly,' Alex says, and grins.

'Butterfly McQueen!' my brother explains. 'From *Gone with the Wind*.'

Gone with the Wind, I understand, is a bad movie. Because my parents have told me, *Gone with the Wind* is racist. But it's on TV all the time. And they can't stop me from watching it when everyone else does. So my parents remind me, frequently: *Gone with the Wind* is a racist movie.

Butterfly McQueen played the slave Prissy in *Gone with the Wind*, a character described in the film as 'a simple minded darky.' When Prissy's owner, the imperious Scarlet, demands that Prissy help her when another woman goes into labour, Prissy, in her childlike voice, confesses her helplessness: 'I don't know nothin' 'bout birthin' babies!'

Who was it who wrote in the 1980s: 'It was preposterous: What young woman raised a slave could have grown up without knowing anything about 'birthin' babies'?'

Alex drops carrots into the big metal juicer. This big and lanky man wearing a flannel shirt, a short Afro – he's the first black man I have ever seen running a health food store.

Who comes in here? A few health food nuts living uptown, Alex's old customers from Harlem.

That's Butterfly.

Butterfly McQueen got her start as a dancer; she danced with the Venezuela Jones Negro Youth Group. She was born with the name Thelma, in Tampa, Florida. Every winter, after she moved to New York City, she would return to the South by bus, making her way to Georgia to wait out the winter. She took the name Butterfly after dancing the Butterfly Ballet in a production of *A Midsummer Night's Dream*.

These are the films and TV shows that Butterfly McQueen appeared in: *The Women, Affectionately Yours, Cabin in the Sky, I Dood It, Flame of Barbary Coast, Mildred Pierce, Duel in the Sun, Killer Diller, Studio One, Beulah, Lux*

Video Theatre, The Green Pastures, The Phynx, Amazing Grace, The Seven Wishes of Joanna Peabody, The Seven Wishes of a Rich Kid, The Adventures of Huckleberry Finn, The Mosquito Coast, and *Polly.*

Malcolm X wrote that, when he watched *Gone with the Wind* and saw Butterfly McQueen doing her Prissy routine, he felt humiliated, 'like crawling under a rug.'

The first four roles Butterfly McQueen accepted after *Gone with the Wind* were maid's roles, she said; then she stopped accepting maid's roles. Years went by. In the *Seven Wishes* films, ABC Afterschool Specials made in the 1970s, she played a fairy godmother referred to as Aunt Thelma. And, in *The Adventures of Huckleberry Finn* – the version made for TV in 1981 – her character was referred to in the credits as Blind Negress.

Butterfly McQueen lived on Sugar Hill. Sugar Hill was where the best known residents of Harlem lived – Paul Robeson, Duke Ellington, and W.E.B Du Bois all once lived there. In 1980, Butterfly McQueen was quoted in the *Palm Beach Post* as saying she was mainly interested in America's black areas. That was to say: she was not interested in the white areas. She recounted her early days touring, how she was forbidden from staying in some of the hotels her troupe visited because she was black.

That's Butterfly.

In 1940, Hattie McDaniel, who plays the slave Mammy in

Gone with the Wind, wins the Oscar for Best Supporting Actress – the first African-American to win an Oscar. She appears at the ceremony in a long-sleeved floor-length gown, a gardenia in her hair and garland of flowers on her shoulder. Her voice quivers while she makes her acceptance speech. Then, she takes her award and returns to the segregated table where she sits, in the back, apart from the film's white cast members.

She goes on to star in *The Male Animal* with Henry Fonda as a domestic worker named Cleota. In *Since You Went Away*, she plays Claudette Colbert's maid, Fidelia. She became the first black star of a radio series, *Beulah*, playing a cook and housekeeper. She plays maids again and again until her death in 1952.

Once Butterfly McQueen decides she will no longer play maids, she is unable to find an acceptable role in a film or TV show for two decades. Instead, she gives music lessons, hosts a radio show, and works at the Stone Mountain Memorial Museum of Confederate Times. She also works as a waitress, a taxi dispatcher, a sales clerk, and a paid companion.

'Was that Butterfly McQueen?'
Alex stands next to the carrot juicer.

In 1980, *People* magazine reports on a lawsuit that Grayhound Bus Lines has settled with Butterfly McQueen after its security guards injured her in a Washington D.C. bus station. The security guards had accused her of being a pickpocket and wrestled her to the ground. This, the article pointed out, happened in spite of the fact that she carried pictures of the stars of *Gone with the Wind* – Clark Gable and Vivien Leigh – with her at all times. The never-married sixty-nine-year-old was a volunteer at her neighborhood school in Harlem, it was noted, and 'into health food these days (grains, nuts, yogurt).'

The bells jingle, and the door swings shut.

'Was that Butterfly McQueen?' my brother asks.

Butterfly McQueen is in the news again in 1989. It's the 50th Anniversary of the release of *Gone with the Wind*, and Butterfly McQueen appears at some of the anniversary celebrations. On stage, in front of adoring audiences, she tells what it was like to appear in the film. She is one of the only surviving cast members.

And Butterfly McQueen recites her most famous line, knowingly: 'I don't know nothin' 'bout birthin' babies.'

Butterfly McQueen dies from injuries sustained in a fire in 1995. In her one-bedroom cottage outside Augusta, a kerosene heater has erupted. She is eighty-four years old. A helium high voice asks: 'Alex, why don't you come back to Harlem?'

The lady in the long skirt turns to leave. The bells on the door play. She wheels her shopping cart outside. The door swings shut.

'Was that Butterfly McQueen?' my brother asks.

Alex glimpses out the door and says: 'That's Butterfly.'

THE PLACE THAT HE CAN NEVER RETURN TO

We're at the exile restaurant on Broadway, the one with darkened windows, and the owner comes out with his slicked down hair and his crisp suit, and he smiles at my father and at me. And I am holding my father's hand, and the owner ruffles my hair and says hello, and in German he welcomes my father. And we go inside, so that my father can tell me about the place that he can never return to.

It smells like roasting beef, vinegar, cucumber, chicken stock, smoked sausage. I will get the knockwurst, because that's just like a hotdog. The waitress, stocky and gray-haired, in her aproned uniform, sees us and nods at my father and smiles down at me and she says,'Hiya, cutie.'

The tables are all covered with crisp linen tablecloths, and the china is white and the glasses curve out and in again. And the waitress always brings me a cup of consommé with little squares of egg noodles. It is never busy at lunch when my father brings me here. Night-time is when people come – my parents, my grandparents, their friends. They sit at a big table in back and they drink Liebfraumilch called Schwarze Katz. There is always a black plastic cat on elastic around the neck of the bottle, and someone always takes it off of the bottle and gives it to me to wear as a bracelet when we're there at night.

· But lunchtime – that's when my father tells me about the place he can never return to.

He says: They lived in a house in a little village. They had a sour cherry tree in the backyard. He used to love sour cherry soup. He knows that sounds strange to me, but if I got to try it, I would understand. His grandfather delivered things from house to house. He had a wagon and it was pulled by a horse. There were farms everywhere there and dogs and cats and hens. It would have been such a good place for me to see.

Outside the horns honk and the cars screech to a stop. You can't see this from the restaurant because the windows are dark. You can't see the graffiti, the soot-darkened apartment blocks, the worn down walk of the workers getting ready to go downtown. You can't see the bodegas, comidas criollas, La Joyeria with big plastic earrings and St. Christopher's medals, and the check cashing stores and the fog-windowed luncheonette.

When the waitress comes, she puts down my knockwurst and potato salad.

And my father asks, 'What do you say to her?'

And I say, 'Danke schön.'

And she says, 'Bitte schön.' And the older people nod, look pleased.

My father picks up the fork, and he says: 'Messer, Gabel, Schere, Licht – gehören in Kinderhände nicht.' He translates: 'Knife, fork, scissors, fire – children must not handle these things.' He gets me to repeat it in German. He smiles when I repeat it. He teaches me how to count in the language he spoke as a child. And I say: 'Ein, zwei, drei, vier, funf…' Up to ten. Once, I even read out loud from *The Aufbau*, the exile newspaper.And he and my mother watch me, beaming.

My father is teaching me the language of a place that he can never return to.

Out on the street, everyone is speaking Spanish, asking 'Que pasa?' and shouting 'Dimelo!' Merengue-swift traffic glides down Broadway, is halted at the crosswalks. The parents are trailing after their kids, exhausted, and the kids are bringing pails and plastic shovels back from the park, complaining about the sand stuck in their pants from the sandbox.

'You wanna know about sand?' someone says in Spanish. 'I'll tell you about sand!'

The parents are telling their kids about the place that they can never return to.

My father sits there with me, in that year before the restaurant closes for good, every day at lunch, teaching me the language that he spoke as a child, a language that only old people speak. He shows me the kind of food he ate as a child: knockwurst, consommé, apple strudel. 'You're going to like this,' he says – 'it's like apple pie.' And when I try it and I tell him I do like it, he grins, relieved.

That place – you know what happened to that place? The building got sold. The RKO cinema next door got turned into Reverend Ike's church. Reverend Ike who preached prosperity consciousness: Why wait 'til you die to get pie in the sky?

The exile restaurant closed. A place opened up next door – they sold automotive equipment, plastic toys. It always smelled like new cars, like vinyl and rubber.

But Spritzer's, the exile restaurant, we used to go there every day. I have a few photos of my parents there, of them with their friends, of the room where they used to drink Liebfraumilch. But there are no other images: no shots of the restaurant from the street, no pictures of the proud owner and waitresses, and nothing showing the tables where my father used to bring me for lunch back then. That was where my father used to tell me about the place that he could never return to.

THIS WAY TO DEPARTURES

I am not surprised when he turns up again. He turns up from time to time. And I agree to him turning up because our relationship was more of a friendship than a romance. And I do not mind meeting him in New York. It's the time of year when I want to get away from the snowplows and sad students. And if I am honest, I will say I am curious. This time, a lot's happened in the interval. This time, I worried about him. This time, I wondered what he was going to do after the elections, whether he could stay in Nicaragua once the Sandinistas were no longer in power. I was expecting to hear from him. We used to joke about it: I was stuck with him.

Danny Rappaport, who I met twenty-five years ago at Columbia, demanding attention from me and everyone else at the anti-war rally: 'Come over here and tell us why the Vietnam War has to end! You – come over here! That's right.' Practically bouncing on the steps of Hamilton Hall while the other students came up and he handed them the megaphone. The policeman's gloved hand closed on his sleeve, and he was pulled down, his hair falling in his eyes. And he looked right at me, and I looked at him, into his amber eyes. When a group of us went to bail the others out, I was hoping I'd see him down at the Tombs. He walked out with the others, rubbing his wrists, flashed me a smile. The ride back uptown, we didn't talk at all, but once we were in the West End Bar, he didn't stop. His dorm-mates told him they were going and he stayed. 'You're not coming home with me,' I warned him. But he did. What a joke. Danny, who couldn't cross the quad without someone running up to him. Everyone thought they were his friend. Danny, who everyone wanted to talk to.

I have always been invisible. I have always been the recipient of half-smiles from people who cannot recall me. I have almost always been ignored.

I liked being alone with my poetry. I read William Carlos Williams over and over.

'I am lonely, lonely.
I was born to be lonely,
I am best so!'

The first time Danny got into my bed, it was because, late at night, we could not stop talking. The second time, there was a shooting down on Amsterdam over heroin and territory and I was too shaken up to be alone that night. And the third time – that was after the great sit-in scam. There was a takeover of Low Memorial and it turned into complete chaos, and Danny said he had to show me something and pulled me out of there. It was a damp spring day. We walked through Central Park, through drizzle and my hair turned curly again. He confessed he couldn't take it anymore – the waiting, the meetings, the confrontations with the cops. He huffed ahead and corralled me into coming along and I saw that we were going toward revolving doors– the Metropolitan Museum of Art. I looked around the big halls, past the guards. He wanted to show me a mural by Diego Rivera, the one of Emiliano Zapata. He wanted to tell me who Rivera was, how he used his art to tell stories about revolution. 'This is just as important as a sit-in,' he reasoned, 'isn't it?' Cold hands under my coat, pulling me to him for a kiss. We never told anyone where we disappeared to that day.

The differences between us were already clear: he waited until the last minute, I always started early; he taunted cops, I lowered my eyes and spoke politely; he left doors open, I always locked them.

I told him I wasn't sure there should be anything beyond a third time, because I knew the kind of life I wanted, and I was not sure it was what he wanted. First of all, there was going to be a house, not some crap apartment like the one where I'd grown up in Washington Heights. A house with a front porch and fireplace and antique furniture that belied the length of my family's time in America. Also, there were going to be meals served on time, with decent food, and no fights that resulted in slammed doors or shouting. Children were going to be treated with respect. I knew all about the sacrifices my mother had made. I knew all about how she'd humored my father, knew all about how she allowed him to believe he was cleverer than he was. Danny had already been back to the Heights with me by then, had already met my father sitting in his stained pants, had already heard my father announce that I was lucky to have gotten Danny. 'He's just a friend,' I said under my breath. Danny lowered his eyebrows then glanced around at thepiles of dirty dishes, the cockroaches, the broken furniture. 'That witch makes me so angry,' my father confessed, when my mother was out of the room. Danny met my eyes, but pretended to my father that he hadn't heard.

'I've got it now,' Danny reassured me, when we were back in my apartment again, in bed.

'Got what?'

'Got why you want what you want. Got why it's important. I'll do it. I'll go along with what you want.'

Anyone could see he wasn't going along with what I wanted... It wasn't what he wanted.

But when he was naked...

It wasn't sexiness that won me over, but his vulnerability.

He'd been born in in Poland. In a displaced persons camp. The war had been over for eighteen months,but his parents couldn't get out of there. The first pictures of him are from that place: his parents holding his arms up as he starts to walk, a sandy-haired toddler in a button-up

shirt and baggy pants, unaware there is any life outside the
camp. In the photograph his parents look older than they
were, but so hopeful. They've survived, married, brought
a son into the world. And they were going to get out. They
were going to go to America, or Canada, or Australia. They
were going to get visas eventually. They were going to
start over. And their son would have no memory of any
of this place. There would only be this photo and what
his parents told him. He would know Evanston, Illinois,
where his parents tried and tried to become middle class
and American. And if they failed,well, they were not the
only ones failing to become happy Americans after the war.

He reached over to touch my hair, and pulled open
a curl and watched it spring together again. We were so
close, I could hear the sound his eyelashes made as they
brushed the pillowcase when he blinked. His face was not
a boy's. He had that big bumpy nose, big sorrowful eyes,
plump gorgeous lips. 'I understand now,' he promised. 'I
know why you want what you want. I'll do it. I'll go along
with what you want.'

I believed him. That night, he convinced me. He convinced
me we could do what out parents could not – have a life
together, have a marriage, a good marriage.

'I am lonely, lonely.
I was born to be lonely,
I am best so!'

I like my crow's feet and the blotches of darkness beneath my eyes, my graying hair, my soft middle and my sagging breasts and my rippled ass. Until I walk into Sparkle and Saint Salon, looking for Aruba conditioner again, and the owner holds up something I don't want.

'No,' I say, shaking my head. 'The one I want is cream something.'

'Cream rinse?' he laughs. He's big with muppety features, can't be much younger than I am. 'That's what they used to call conditioner a long time ago. This is conditioner.'

On a lower shelf, I find it: Aruba Cream Reconstruction. 'This is what I was looking for,' I say.

'Oh that.'

Then, to a restaurant to meet a friend, where the waiter calls us 'young ladies' all night and smiles, as if we should be flattered by his condescension.

Then my teaching assistant arrives at my house, delivering the quizzes she's graded for the course, and she oohs and aahs over the polished wood, the big-windowed rooms, and the plump furniture. 'Wow,' she says. 'It's huge! How many people live here?'

And her big brown eyes flattening, her little mouth opening.

The unsaid word: Alone?

I am best so.

Danny and I bought the house when he was at Harvard, when Somerville was still called Slummerville. And that student who oohed and aahed over my house – she would have been afraid of coming here at all in those days.

I worked on the house during weekends. I blasted the walls back to brick. I scraped off yellow and pink flowered wallpaper. I soaked years of paint off the wood trim. Danny would be in his office, at his advisor's house, in Poland on a Fulbright. He'd return and I would pull down the bandanna I had tied over my mouth to keep the dust out. 'You look like Che Guevara doing home repairs,' he told me, once. He'd drop his bags on the floor, half-unpack, go into the bedroom to make phone calls. Danny, walking around the house, taking a bite of an apple, reading the mail while he stood at the table.

I stripped the cracked linoleum. The wood floors gleamed. I'd brought a museum-heavy table home on the roof of the red Datsun. I had never lived anywhere as beautiful or solid as that house. Danny? He treated it like a stopover, another hotel, someplace to retool before he went out again.

He was published, celebrated, quoted. His first book was hot explanations of IMF economics, stories about people living under the IMF's austerity measures: diets of boiled rice, sweatshops substituting for schools, dysentery-wracked children. That book became the staff recommendation in university town bookstores all over America. Critics called it propaganda, said his arguments were manipulative, inaccurate, unbalanced. Even supporters admitted his ideas were not entirely original. It was the way he conveyed them that earned him accolades. He was accessible, moving, funny. He was funniest when he was angry. He had a string of jokes about the World Bank. He swaggered into the lecture hall, paced like a stand-up comedian. Socialism, supply-side, and here's the punch line. I was proud of him, but I could see where it all was going.

I sat in on a few of his talks and couldn't help laughing, even though I'd heard him say it all before. The others in the lecture mistook me for a student. I was thirty-two years old by then, was teaching a full load of literature and women's studies, was up for tenure. The mistake must have come from the lack of authority I had. I'd given up the offer from Stanford so that Danny could accept his offer from Harvard. And I was lucky to find a teaching post in the same town as him, so how could I say no to small, pretty, second choice Chestnut College?

And then came the Nicaraguan Revolution – 1981, and there were stories in *Time*, in *Newsweek*. The very first articles were about the overthrow of Somoza and the new transitional government. Initially the coverage seemed hopeful – the war was over and the dictator had finally been defeated. But now, the news magazine said, it appeared the new government was in league with the Eastern Bloc, was in fact totalitarian. Danny was one of the academics invited to Nicaragua by the new government. Would he like to come see for himself? Perhaps he could deliver a few lectures at the university in Managua. He could also visit some of the collective

farms that had just been formed. He could see what was
possible now that the people were free to realize the
hopes that they had harbored all this time.

Danny's first phone calls home cracked with emotion,
broke into disjointed phrases because of bad connections.
They were like combustion engines, driven by little
explosions. The Sandinistas had launched a literacy
campaign, dispatched young people across the country to
teach rural workers to read and write. The land was going
to belong to those workers. Big estates were about to be
nationalized. Collectives were springing up on the farms that
the landowners had left behind. But the CIA was beginning
to arm former National Guardsmen, and a war was starting
up again. He would fight them, I thought he told me. He
was going to stay there, with the Sandinistas, and fight.

The line was crackling.

We lost the connection.

I wasn't able to give him the news I had.

Classes had already started when Danny returned to
Boston. I couldn't go to meet him at the airport. I had a
seminar to lead. He was waiting at home for me when I
was done. It was an unusually cold September day. Leaves
were stirring in the driveway. Inside, he had a fire going.
His face was brown from the sun and his eyes were shining.
He leapt up when he saw me, took me in his arms, gave me
more of a clinch than an embrace. At first I half-believed he
knew what I was going to tell him, sensed it. But he hadn't

of course. His anticipation – the way he held his breath, watched me carefully, and could barely sit – all that was there because *he* had something to tell *me*.

He understood now where he was supposed to be, he said in a rush. He had never seen any place like Nicaragua. It was a place where the best parts of socialism could finally be put into action. He was going back there. He was going to take a leave of absence from Harvard. He was going to write about Sandinista economic policies. And I – I was going to love it there. I would see how beautiful the country was. There were poets in the government, poets everywhere. I would learn Spanish quickly. After all, hadn't I already learned some growing up where I did? I could stop teaching the rich college students I'd always complained about and teach there instead! They would love me. I would love them. He understood now that America was not going to have a revolution after all – but Nicaragua – they had one now. And that's where we were going to live.

I had news too.

I was ten weeks pregnant.

Danny's mouth opened slightly, and he let out a little gasp, but no words came out. His eyes welled up with tears. I stopped breathing.

The logs in the fireplace glowed red, grayed down.

He blinked, and his eyes stayed damp, but he didn't cry.

We were never going to have children together.

I cried.

I wept for two whole days.

I wept while he asked me: 'How can we do this now?'

I wept while he comforted me.

I wept when he told me it was okay and reassured me that I could have the baby in Nicaragua.

I wept while he yelled: 'How can you actually think about having this baby?'

And I wept all the way to the abortion clinic. They advised me to wait.

I didn't want to.

They asked me if I was certain.

I was certain.

It was the end of the first trimester by then.

He left in January 1982.

'I'm there whenever you want to come,' he told me.

Summer came, and I rebuilt the back porch, took out the rotting floorboards and replaced them with fresh lumber. I put some flower boxes on the railing: verbena, lantana, fuschia. I put a wicker chair on the porch and brought a wrought-iron table out there.

The US began mining Nicaragua's harbors that year. Everyone knew the CIA helped lay the mines – it was in all the American papers. The mines weren't big enough to sink the ships in the harbor, but they made it risky to sail in and out – coffee and other exports began piling up on the piers. Imported oil ran short. The war was growing. Danny was visiting a co-operative farm when it was attacked. Boys and men were taken by the Contras. A family that resisted was murdered in front of the others – with machetes. The stock of corn was set alight, and the fires spread to the wooden shacks that the families lived in.

Danny returned to Boston for a speaking engagement. When he showed slides of the co-operative ravaged by the war, he began shaking. There was something in him that hadn't been there before – hope replaced by rage. The students watched him, listened to him, in awe. I wanted to get him out of there. And I couldn't help myself – he wound up back in my bed that night. And when the thunderstorm began at 2 AM, he scrambled down to the floor, flattened himself to avoid fire. I sat up, pulled the covers over my knees, and looked out the window thinking: *This is your life now.*

The houses next door were briefly illuminated every time the lightning cracked down. Were the families in them living lives they were happy with? I didn't think so. I'd seen women worry about whether they were going to marry, worry about whether they'd have kids before time ran out, and then fester with resentment, complaining they didn't even feel their bodies were their own anymore. I'd seen their husbands appearing briefly to hint at their own misery. And whenever I saw any of this, I was always happy to go back to my own home. Lightning cracked, and thunder roared, and the heaviness lifted, and I could breathe. And I knew how the rest of my life would play out. I would have none of what the others were having.

Danny and I divorced in August that year.

Terminal 8 is where splashes of red and blue boomerang across an enormous stained-glass window, an old-fashioned idea of what was modern, from the days of American optimism, when the airport was called Idlewild instead of JFK in honor of an assassinated president. We stand in open coats, hats stuffed into our pockets – the welcoming committee for New York's winter. The passengers arriving are dressed for hot weather – shorts, sandals, halter dresses and big earrings. And heeeeyyyy and looook and miiiirra! Everyone's calling out to their parents, their kids, their cousins. They recognize one another, freeze, then rush to each other – propelled, desperate, animated. What will I do? What will I say to a man I haven't seen in almost ten years? My nerves almost kept me from making it in time. I was in the wrong part of the terminal, unable to find arrivals before I realized that, all along, I had done what I do automatically when I arrive at an airport alone. I made my way to departures.

Which version of Danny should I look for here? Dark and pot-bellied? Wizened and old? Bald and baseball-capped?

And then I see him, plump and sun-darkened, hair grayer but he has all of it and he looks more familiar than he ever has, more familiar than the last time I saw him. He hoists his bags easily, and gazes into the crowd, but he doesn't see me. Does he not recognize who I am now? I call out his name and he turns and then he does see, and his smile is enormous, and he rushes toward me and drops his bags and pulls me close. I smell his sweat, the cotton of his t-shirt, and the clean residue of shaving cream. And it all comes back – Columbia, the overheated apartment where I lived in Spanish Harlem, the drive to Boston that first time, me thinking Boston is far away from where I'm from and it is nothing like New York, it is houses and trees and a crazy little subway line where everything is named after a color like a crayon, and we will live the rest of our lives here having escaped. It all comes rushing back as he pulls me close, holds me, kisses the top of my head. And I hear a man observe, in a smug Southern accent, 'Now there's a man who's happy to see his wife.'

The drive into the city is snow-snarled, lanes of cars converging in an angry stream, honking horns and spat curses. I'm trying to tell Danny where we're going. I'm trying to tell him about the borrowed apartment on West 104th, Maureen's. I wonder if he'll remember Maureen.

But Danny just mumbles a distracted, 'Okay.'

He's looking out the window, brow furrowed. 'Why are there so many cars?'

'It's New York. It's a traffic jam.'

He stares and stares, starts to say something, stops. Then his jaw drops and his eyes water, and reaches up and pushes his fingers against his eyes.

'Danny?' I ask.

'There aren't that many cars in Nicaragua,' he explains. 'Because of the war.'

'I know,' I tell him quickly, to make him stop.

The apartment is cramped, dusty, overheated, filled with worn furniture and piles of books, comforting. There's a threadbare Oriental rug on the floor and windowsills decked with neglected plants, an overfed cat that eyes us with suspicion.

I've got a coat for Danny, one he left at the house a long time ago – North Face, navy blue, barely worn. He laughs when he sees it and tries it on. It's tighter than it should be, but it fits.

He looks up at the sky when we leave the building, theatrically takes in the scene around him. But once we get down to Broadway, he starts bumping into people. He apologizes, but then he does it again. And the racks outside the novelty shops make him stare: foam Statue of Liberty hats, beepers that hang on your belt, t-shirts with a pop-eyed yellow cartoon character. He has never seen any of these things before. As we make our way south, the shops start to look glossier and the people better dressed. Ninety-sixth Street has always been a border of sorts. Danny wants to know who the cartoon character is. I tell him about *The Simpsons*: about Bart, about his mother Marge who has a blue bouffant and his father Homer who works in a nuclear power plant. Bart Simpson is the most popular character on television, I add. Danny's eyes narrow. Am I serious? Yes, I nod, I am. Danny turns when he hears a horn honk, when he hears someone shout in Spanish. Pigeons rise on the traffic island. And we reach Zabar's, Zabar's with its loaves of bread and baskets of cookies and jars of olives displayed in its big plate glass windows.

I ask if he wants to go inside and when we do, we ogle the bagels, bread in the shape of moons, challah with shiny tops covered with poppy seeds. Danny is paralyzed and then entranced by the glass refrigerators filled with cheeses, cold cuts, salads decorated with capers.

'The supermarkets are empty in Managua,' he reports, reaching inside one of the refrigerators. 'You can find an entire aisle of vodka and Russian sardines.'

'That sounds like a great diet,' I tell him.

I hand him a shopping basket. He fills it with lox, pate, raisin black bread, brie, potato salad with dill, artichoke spread, brioche, whitefish.

Then he stops, looking down at the basket.

'I'll get it,' I confirm.

The table is piled high with papers and books, so we decide to have a picnic in the living room: we spread a tablecloth onto the floor. We scatter the plastic containers on top of it, open a bottle of cheap red wine, pour it into water-spotted blue wine glasses. Danny is on his knees, falls back awkwardly, surprisingly childlike in his jeans. Suddenly I glimpse him as a toddler again, displaced, trying to walk for his parents.

'How long are you here for?' I ask.

'Good question,' he replies.

'Where do you have to be after this?'

'I don't have to be anywhere,' he says.

I must have let go of my glass, because suddenly a puddle

of red wine is spreading beneath me. Nothing shattered – just a big, red stain soaking into the rug.

'Shit!' I shout.

I run to the small, messy kitchen searching for something to wipe up the wine, pull a roll of paper towels from a cheap plastic dispenser on the wall.

Danny takes the paper towels from me, blots the wine, his expression grave. I go to get a sponge and squeeze some dishwashing liquid onto it, then rub that against the rug too. In the end, there is a pale pink blotch beneath us, beaded gray shreds of paper towel everywhere.

Danny refills my glass. I turn and look out the window. Huge snowflakes are falling from a dead steel-colored sky, down past the brick, down to the street where they never last for more than a few seconds before the traffic turns them to slush.

Danny is standing beside me as if he has never left – solid, attentive, and, as always, just a bit damaged. And yet there is something fundamentally different about him, about his body language – bigger, more directive, than it was the last time I saw him. In some way, he has become Nicaraguan.

'Why did you leave?' I ask him.

'I didn't leave. I asked you to come with me.'

My mouth opens a little. 'You know that's not what I meant. Why did you leave Nicaragua?'

'It's all over,' he says.

And when I say nothing, he confirms: 'The end of the revolution.'

I take a sip of my wine. He looks away from me – out the window.

'Was she Nicaraguan?' I ask.

He turns back to me.

'The one you just broke up with.'

He doesn't answer, but I can see that I'm on to something.

'She broke up with *you*?' I say.

He puts his glass on the edge of a bookshelf.

'She's American.'

'The one you called a war junkie in your email?'

'I was upset when I wrote that.'

'Right out of college?'

'She's twenty-eight. A journalist.'

'And you're here because...'

'I didn't leave because of her. I couldn't renew my residency permit.'

'Because of the new government?'

He nods.

'What are you going to do?' I ask.

'I don't know,' he admits.

We go walking. Because what else do you do when you don't know what to do? He and I decide to walk downtown, out in the snow and in the dark of the early nightfall. We walk past the canopy-fronted buildings of Central Park West. We walk past the Museum of Natural History. We walk down to Central Park South, with its horse-drawn carriages and an ugly black glass tower named after a real estate tycoon.

Some kids appear, two boys and a girl in cheap nylon parkas, skipping ahead of their big tired parents who made the subway trip to see the department store windows and Christmas lights. The boy jumps up and down and in Uptown vowels hollers: 'Look at the horse! Ma! Look at the horse! Look at it!'

'I've memorized it already,' she shouts back.

And the boy scampers to her, comforted by the insult. And she puts her arms around him. She says something to the boy that I can't hear, and they laugh, and then the boy goes running off again.

'You still think of having children?' Danny asks.

'I'm forty-four years old,' I remind him.

Danny's hands are shoved into his pockets. The clop clop of hooves seems loud for a moment. Then a taxi, headlights on bright, slaps a puddle of slush into the air. Danny pulls me back. His arms stay around me.

Snow falls. It stays on Danny's brown hair, melts when it reaches his sun-dark skin.

'Aren't you cold?' I ask.

'No,' he says.

I step away from his hold.

'Let's go to Rockefeller Center,' he says.

'Rockefeller Center?'

'I want to show you something.'

A few more blocks and we reach it: the tree towering and all lit up, the ice-skating rink and the professional skaters mixing in with the amateurs. And it is – all of it – something from the past, something your parents would take you to, something the city celebrated when there was less there, less to do. The beaux arts building is from when Manhattan was building and rebuilding; when its spiky skyline spread, a landscape under construction that mimicked the groves of towers in *Metropolis*. A statue of the Angel Gabriel seems to hover over the ice, as if it's going to fly. Tourists throng, and in the rink, women wearing red felt skirts glide, arms out, jubilant, looking up at the crowds. On the edge of the rink, hanging onto the walls and barely managing to stay upright, are the families having their weekend in New York – a girl on the verge of tears, her father speaking to her sternly, the mother standing by and watching.

'What are you thinking about?' Danny asks.

'About my parents,' I say. 'They used to bring me here. We never did anything but watch. It was a big day out for them, and it always ended with my father shouting. And I'm thinking about how I swore I would never be like them.'

He reaches up and unfurls one of my curls.

'You know they finally got a divorce in the Seventies because it was alright to get a divorce then?' I remind him. 'You remember that?'

His mouth opens slightly, but he waits for me to go on.

'And you remember how they got married again ten years later? Everyone acted like it was such a good thing?'

He swallows like a frightened boy, then turns away from me, toward the ice rink.

I conclude: 'It wasn't a good thing.'

Danny says, under his breath, 'You're not like them.'

He's looking at the skaters, at the angel, at the building

behind. A woman starts gliding backwards, her arms open as if she's expecting applause. A suburban father crashes into her. They grab each other, apologising.

'You know Diego Rivera painted a mural in there?' Danny asks.

'Where?'

'Right there.'

'In Rockefeller Center?'

'Rockefeller hired Diego Rivera to paint a mural. When this building was first built.'

'Where?'

'Right there in the lobby. Rivera was – you know – really big back then.'

'What about his politics? Didn't that bother Rockefeller?'

'Rivera was one of the biggest artists in world, so Rockefeller hired him. And this mural was supposed to have everything in it – war and industry and agriculture. And Rivera put a labor leader in the middle bringing everyone together, which in and of itself doesn't seem like a bad thing. But then the thing was almost finished. And then you could see the labor leader had a little pointy beard and glasses. It was Lenin.'

'This really happened?' I ask.

'Yes, it really happened,' Danny laughs. 'So Rockefeller goes nuts and tells Rivera to repaint it. But Rivera... You know, he's Rivera. He says it's his vision, it's his painting. Lenin's going to stay in the the mural. So, one night, Rockefeller's workmen come in, and they chisel the mural off the wall.'

'What?'

'They chisel the mural off the wall,' Danny repeats. 'They take it right out of the building and they throw it into the trash.'

'You're kidding me.'

Danny's grinning. His eyes shine. There's that look he gets when he has an audience. 'I'm not kidding you. And then Rockefeller brings in another artist to repaint the wall.'

'So that's the mural that's in there now? The second mural?'

Danny nods. 'And Rivera goes back to Mexico,' he says, 'and he paints the mural he wanted all over again in Mexico City in the Palace of Fine Arts. Only this time, Rockefeller's in the middle of it. And there's a sign that says "Smash Rockefeller Serfdom."'

Danny steps behind me, and he puts a hand on either side of me, and he pulls me close. He wraps his arms around me from behind.

And I can't speak.

The snow falls, filling the silence between us with more silence. I stare at Rockefeller Center, imagining that small amount of time after most of Rivera's mural was painted, before Rockefeller had it destroyed.

It was like that between Danny and me, that small amount of time, that night I heard his eyelashes brush the pillowcase. I knew what I wanted and did not want. Nothing – nothing – seemed as glorious to me as autonomy. I'd taken him to meet my parents, a living example of why we were going to go separate ways. He was going to take the post-doc at Harvard, and I was going to go to Berkeley where everyone I'd ever wanted to work with taught. But I was, finally, persuaded to settle down. Not comrades, not lovers any longer, but husband and wife – a marriage neither of us ever quite managed to get out of again.

'I know why you want what you want,' he said.

But he didn't. Not really, because he didn't think the thing I wanted really mattered.

He offered me this other thing, which was what everyone told me I should want. He offered me a kind of marriage that was not unlike the kind that other women had.

We were so close, I could hear the sound his eyelashes made as they brushed the pillowcase when he blinked. 'I understand now,' he promised. 'I know why you want what you want. I'll do it. I'll go along with what you want.'

He convinced me we could have a life together, have a marriage, a good marriage. I believed him. That night, he convinced me.

FACSIMILES

At night the buildings return, silvery and solid and rising, filling in the space left in the skyline. They are monsters of steel and shine, floor after floor of metal desks and castered chairs and fuzz-frothed cubicles buzzing with electricity and language.

The first time the buildings returned, I was in a yoga class, and suddenly, they were present. It was evening by then and the buildings shined in the distance. I could see them from the studio window. The smell from the fire was gone – no melted plastic, molten glass, scorched steel. The few of us who had made it to yoga class were chanting for peace, and then for true identity – we chanted, sat nam sat nam sat nam. We sat with legs folded and eyes closed.

Then, I was no longer in the room. It was not night, but the middle of the day. It was a few weeks before it happened. I was in the plaza – the enormous plaza between the buildings. There was summer heat, but not actual sun. The sun always struggled to get its place there. The neighborhood, built almost entirely in the late nineteenth century, always looked like an old stained photograph, existed in sepia. And there, in the middle of all those fussy old office buildings, in that place that still looked as if it should have been inhabited by men in waistcoats and bowler hats, stood those 1970s slabs of glass and light, arrogant and big and so optimistic about the future. Those towers embodied the Seventies, designed by people too wrapped up in the moment to know how ugly the buildings would appear later on, how obsolete they would become soon after their construction.

But I was in the plaza at noon, beneath the buildings' hulking shadows. Everything was as it had been before, and I was waiting for Inez to meet me for lunch. I was sitting on the cement step that dipped into the plaza. And everywhere, there were people waiting, or eating hot dogs, or reading newspapers. Pigeons fluttered in for scraps. And there was a boy nearby, perhaps a college student, perhaps the son of an executive. He had tousled hair and wore a too-large Oxford cloth shirt, the tie pulled loose and the collar undone. Since it was summer, there were many interns trying out jobs on Wall Street. And there were students taking on temp jobs, jobs of frustration and photocopies.

But this boy, with his tousled hair and his expensive clothes, he was not someone who would stay there in a terrible job in the copier room. Already, he was preparing his costume. He took a cigar from his shirt pocket, put it in his mouth, and lit it. Then, with his thumb and forefinger, he removed the cigar from his mouth, and his lips, pale and delicate, pursed with disgust. He looked so ridiculous there, as he tried to smoke, that I narrowed my eyes and grinned – this boy, with a child's face, wishing he were a man with a cigar. I thought, this is the sort of asshole Inez will be working for one day. Ten summers from now, he will be a rising manager and she will be his assistant. And I could smell the air – that's how real it was. I could inhale that downtown air when it still smelled like downtown: exhaust, and roast sugared nuts, and hot concrete, and, yes, just the tiniest trail of cigar smoke.

I burst into tears. It was not noon, but night; not the middle of summer, but nearly fall. And the buildings, of course, were gone, had been gone since two days before. In their place were ruins – glass, metal, bodies. In their place was rising smoke, still flames, and funeral pyres. The plaza was filled with ash. Ash was falling everywhere. Even on us, miles from there, across the river.

But the buildings, in mid-September, were present to me. I kept my eyes closed and felt the tears run quickly down my face, one after the other. And I lifted my hand from my knee to wipe my face, then regained the pose. I felt the footsteps of my yoga teacher come close, then heard her pass. I was glad she had gone and let me be.

I wasn't a photocopy clerk by design, but had become one by default. It was the only thing that I could stand to do

and it was the only thing that my employers could stand
to have me doing. Weeks after beginning work at Stevens
Brothers Investing (Tower One, 47th floor), weeks after
they became aware of the wrongly routed phone messages,
slow typing, and 'uncongenial demeanor,' I was reassigned
to the copy room. Down the long hallway, second left, third
right, through swinging doors (not the glass doors), past
the vending machines, second left again, and then don't
go *through* the next set of swinging doors – bear left so that
you go past them – and, kitty corner to the ladies room
(but not easy to see, because of a new row of cubicles that's
sprung up), there it is: the copy room! Because I did not
have the skills required to be an administrative assistant,
and because I was unwilling to wear appropriate attire for
the office (opaque hosiery was excluded from the office dress
code), the copy room seemed like the best place to put me.

You knew me. You used to pass me in the hall and nod and
smile, good you, who even knew the names of the mailroom
clerks and the boys in the copy rooms. When you saw us
on the street, in the beginning of the shadowed light on
Cortlandt or on Varick Street, you kept your head down and
walked a little quickly, a little fearfully, especially if there was
no one else on the street. And then you'd see it was one of us
– from work, from Stevens Brothers Investing's copy room
or mailroom, and you'd nod and smile with relief. Because,
that's right, you knew me. You knew me, standing in there
and that room with its constant shuffle of paper flying from

the sorter and dropping into its stacks, rhythmic clicking of the electric stapler, constant hum. Loud hum, loud shuffle, so that after you'd waited your turn and you'd come up to the window holding your stack of papers (you in your business suit, me in my t-shirt and jeans), you'd have to shout when you went over your order with me. *And I want them spiral bound, back to back, and – I'm sorry – but can you have it done by four o'clock this afternoon?* Pleading smile, pleading tilt of your head, pleading with me to please get it done by this afternoon, even if it meant putting your order ahead of everyone else's, so you could get back at a decent hour that night, go back to your family in Parsippany, or Harrison, or Rye. You'd give me that ingratiating smile to see if I'd help you, hoping I wouldn't do the things to your order that I did to your coworkers who I didn't like – reinvent the chronology of pages, leave the charts that are referred to out, insist the order was never brought in, and only after true panic and hysteria sets in say, *Oh, here it is. I see. Sorry.* No, I wouldn't do that to you. You were the decent one.

You knew me.

And you knew why I was never fired, why I still came in, day after day, showing my ID to security, passing through the metal detector, squeezing into the elevator as it sped up and up and up, passing my vinyl-coated key card before the double set of glass-topped doors until they buzzed open. You knew me. And I even knew you: Miriam Borcher, Managing Director of Administration for Global Fixed Income, with your dowdy suits and your gimp foot and your speech impediment, snubbed so often you couldn't stand to fire anyone. Eventually, you were fired though, and, then I was too.

I slept after the yoga class. Inez didn't. And when I woke on Friday morning, she was staring out of the window, out at the gray that was never going to lift. From our living room window, above the forest of buildings, we'd been able to see the top of the World Trade Center, our distance from the towers shrinking them to a manageable size. Big silver rectangles, always hulking. Inside them, I was reminded repeatedly of my insignificance. Remember the blocks those buildings spanned, the offices with floor space so wide and so circuitously furnished, that getting lost was common? I hated those buildings the way you hate a drunk and widowed uncle who moves in with your family. How could you get away from them? How could you show that they had nothing to do with you at all?

I was lucky in more ways than one. After I was fired, I got a job with Downtown Copies. A lot less money, and a lot less misery, I didn't dread my workday anymore.

Inez was in the easy chair when I woke up, the old lumpy one, staring at the spot where the towers should have been, at the rising smoke, the yellow air. We both stared at the emptiness.

'Are you going?' Inez asked. 'To work today?'

'I have to go,' I explained to her. 'You know, it's crazy there now. I'm sorry, honey.'

She had her knees drawn up and a pillow clutched to her chest, was wearing an old t-shirt and sweatpants. Inez, purple under her eyes and shadowed face, still looking like a little girl in all her misery. Her hair fell in curls that always made people think she was younger, and kinder, than she actually was. She got away with everything at Stevens Brothers. The Riot Grrls 'zines I used to run off for her in the copy room were just the start of it. She kept on there after I was fired, and it caused only a little irritation between us. After all, she had the administrative assistant scam down pat. From the Stevens Brothers offices, she surreptitiously managed marketing for half the artists in Williamsburg. On the day that it happened, she hadn't made it into work yet. But I didn't know that, didn't find that out until noon, after the towers had fallen, when she made it up to 14th Street and Downtown Copies.

Crazy there.

MISSING
Vittorio (Vic) Genoroso
Worked for Cantor Fitzgerald
Last seen on 97th floor.
Any information please call: 917-555-3535

MISSING FROM WTC 1, 106th Floor
This is my sister, Shaniqua Lennox. She worked for Windows on the World. She is 5' 3", and weighs 135 lbs. You can't see it in this picture, but she has a mole on her left shoulder, her hair is shorter now. Her friends call her Shanny. She's diabetic and needs her medication.

If you see her, please follow her. She may have amnesia.
Please call me at 718-553-2312 (home) or 917-555-
6845 (cell)

Vanava Singh vital statistics
Born May 17, 1963 38 years old
5'7", 160 – 170 lbs
Has tattoo of butterfly on her ankle. No piercings.
Wearing antique gold locket, blue and green
Swatch watch, and a traditional wedding band.
Last seen 9/11/01 approximately 8 AM leaving
from Path train to the towers.
Last wearing beige jacket, white shirt, long
flowered skirt.
If anyone has ANY information about her, please
call Nezam Singh: 201-555-2211 or 917-555-
9332

Have you seen this person?
Javier Antonio Fernandez
22 years old
Delivering package to Stonefield Trust on 57th
Floor.
Please!!! Call us!!! 718-555-8385

Missing
Please help
Joseph Zinzi
Globo Brokers

Please call 718-555-2142
God and Angels up above, send us home the one
we love.

I scan their pictures into the Mac so they copy evenly with
no puddling of toner – the man with the sunglasses grinning
in a dark suit, the woman in a sleeveless and glittery dress
at a party. I crop the picture of the woman and her sister
so that only the face of the missing shows. This is what her
sister asks if I can do when she comes in, voice husky when
she tells me what she wants while she pulls things out of her
shoulder bag. *Oh my God, where did I put it?* Out comes tape,
rumpled forms to be filled out, a notebook, photos, all onto
the countertop. *Oh my God. Oh my God. Here it is. You can just
focus in on her face? It won't get too blurry?*

All day long, I scan and I copy. I call Inez every couple of
hours. *Hey baby, you okay? Whyn't you try to sleep a little?* She
says a neighbor's visiting, and I'm happy she's with someone.
A copier jams. And behind us, people are lining up, waiting
to make their missing posters. They go out in the rain, into
the air that smells like burning plastic and rubber, and they
hold the posters against the buildings with the heels of their
hands and they try to make the posters stick. The sirens wind
up the air and let it fall in yellow again. The rain drives down
the ashes. The only comforting sound is the familiar choong
choong choong of the copy machines, the choong choong
choong and the paper flying out. Except that the paper keeps
flying out with pleas for help to find the missing. Choong
choong choong. Last seen on 86th floor. Choong choong

choong. Called and left message right after Tower One was hit. Choong choong choong. Nickname is Didi.

The door slams open, letting a gust of rubbery-smelling wind into the copy shop, where too many people have squeezed inside – there are too many people working behind the counter, and too many people waiting. A man stands just inside the doorway, wire-rimmed glasses and plaid shirt, blinking, disoriented. *You make free copies?*

We can make posters for you if you're trying to find someone. We don't charge anything for that. And, because he still hesitates: *You can come in.*

He enters, lets the door shut behind him.

From his ratty old backpack, he takes out a small photograph, still in its frame, of a shirtless man with dark eyes smiling shyly, squinting into the sun, ocean behind him. He flips the frame over, starts to undo the clips against its cardboard backing. Then he turns away, hands flying to his face, sobbing.

Inez is watching TV when I return, in the same t-shirt and pajama bottoms she was wearing that morning. The lights are dim. Blue television light bleats against her shadowed face. She turns to me, then pulls an afghan up that's slipped from the sofa to the floor. She asks, *Was it okay out there?*

I've never seen anything like this, I tell her. *Everyone's crying and being so nice.*

No response from her. She looks at me as if I have said all this in a language she doesn't understand.

So I try for an old line, one I use when we're out of the city and missing New York: *I just keep wishing someone would bump into me and tell me to fuck off.*

She turns back to the TV. On screen, they're showing it again: an airplane shooting into the tower, a plume of smoke blossoming, the fire beginning again. On screen, smoke is consuming the building, wind is pushing the smoke from its column. The building is gone.

Silently, Inez begins to weep.

She puts her hands over her face, convulsing. I put the bag of Chinese food I've brought onto the coffee table, slide next to her on the vinyl couch. I take her in my arms, bony, damp from tears and sweat, flannel brushing my arm and afghan crumpled between our thighs. She quivers against me, against my chest and the cotton of my shirt, then stops weeping and picks at one of my buttons, a sick little girl. *I keep wishing only I felt this bad,* she says. *I keep wishing this were just happening to me.*

I know, I tell her, because I can think of nothing else to say.

I look over her shoulder, out the window. And there, above the brownstones and churches of Brooklyn, over on the Manhattan side, there they are – two rectangles of steel, the buildings.

I think, this must be some kind of optical illusion. This must be some freak reflection of searchlights, some unknown effect.

And I rise.

I stand by the window, fingertips against cool glass. If I stare long enough, these buildings will disintegrate. The shine will fall away. The shape will blur.

My heart pounds. I smell moo shoo chicken. But a burning smell – plastic, bodies, static – laces underneath the smell of food.

I know, Inez says, turning to me now. *I just keep looking out there. It's like I'm trying to get that this really happened, that they're gone.*

Their geometric light cuts through the yellow-tinted air. They are there.

She falls asleep in my arms, stirs when I try to shift. So I lie there, neck aching because I can't move, me awake this time – we take turns.

I wonder sometimes if we'll ever want sex again, or if it will just be this: holding each other and being grateful I'm not alone.

It's only been four days since the world has been this way, but most of the time I feel as if there was nothing before this and will be nothing after – no jumping out of the bushes to surprise her in the park, no making fun of tourists, no laughing. And fuck all this talk about America losing its innocence. Who's innocent? It wasn't like we didn't know how ugly the world really was. We knew. We just didn't feel it every day, all the time. There was drinking cheap sake at Decibel, and scamming tickets from our friend who worked at Town Hall, and punching holes in the ice over puddles while we waited for the bus at Union Square. It wasn't innocence exactly. It was more like making the most of what was there.

Did we think about how we were exempt from what people in rest of the world were dealing with? Sometimes.

Some of us. And were we grateful that this place we lived in was safe in some way? Sometimes. Some of us. Now all of it looks like the good old days. Now all of it glows like lights on Christmas Eve. *And I in my nightshirt, and ma in her cap.* Even waiting for the St. Nicholas Avenue bus at one AM and knowing it might never come. Even stuck uptown after visiting childhood friends. Even shoved in the subway and...

I wish someone would tell me to fuck off.

On an ordinary day, there'd be me and Inez negotiating over who got to use the shower first, shoving things aside to search for clean clothes, walking wet-haired down to Fourth Avenue, clutching our scratched plastic coffee-filled cups. Fourth Avenue, where most mornings we went together to the subway station for the N, the R, and the F trains – the Never, the Rarely, and the Fucked. Seventh Avenue was suburban suck-ups, Ivy League fat asses that sat in brownstones restored to their former grandeur. They emerged dressed in t-shirts that read: Brooklyn, Only the Strong Survive. And most of the people on that side of the Slope who looked like Inez and me were pushing strollers with white triplets inside and left the neighborhood after dark. But Fourth Avenue, that was ours – with its boarded-up buildings and derelict storefronts. I was always comforted by its blight. And then Inez and I would wait for the N or the R. We always had to stand, hanging onto the pole with one hand while we shared the paper. She'd get off at Cortlandt Street. We'd kiss each other goodbye, and I'd ride up to Union Square. And why does that seem like it was such an intimate thing, her with her morning sleepiness kissing me goodbye at Cortlandt Street?

The subways bypass that now. There is no stop, no station there anymore.

Suddenly I remember another joke: Big blizzard, 1996. Subways barely running, but a few lines still go. The Mayor has declared the city shut down. Inez gets a call from Stevens Brothers. She's expected to come into work.

They'd expect you in the day after a nuclear holocaust, I said then. Haha.

I shift my arm. She stirs, pushes me back, in her sleep, against the bed.

I want to see if the towers are there, but I can't get the right angle out the window from where I lie. I can't move.

🔽

The phones. I haven't mentioned the phones. Dead silence in the building, and then, all at once, they ring. *No, no. We're fine. We weren't anywhere near it. Yeah. I know. In shock.*

An orchestra of voices: Spanish, Kreyol, Hebrew. Signaling reassurance any way you can.

Inez's mother calls from Puerto Rico. Mine's just uptown, just in the Heights, but she calls too and puts all the relatives and neighbors on.

And then, the long lost start to get in touch – emails and phone messages from people I barely knew before:

Hi, Ani. It's Mavis. I know it's been awhile.

Ani, howya doin'? It's Tony. Listen, I'm living in New Haven now. You okay? You can come stay with us if you want.

Hey, girl. I just want to see if you're alright. Just call and tell me you're okay. Okay? I just want you to know I'm thinking of you.

Thinking of you. Worried about you. Know that you work there. Wondering where you are. Please call. Praying for you. Praying for all of us. This isn't World War Three, is it? Missing you. So sad. So stunned. So sick. So fucked up. Praying. I just wanted to hear your voice. Crying. Love you. Please call. Praying.

CNN. The faces of the dead suspects arranged on the TV screen.

The president's inane declarations:

We will rid the world of the evildoers. We will call together freedom loving people to fight terrorism.

To hunt down, to find, to smoke out of their holes the terrorist organization that is the prime suspect.

This crusade, this war on terrorism is going to take a while.

And shit, Inez, can't you turn that off? I call out to her, *I'm trying to talk to my brother in Chicago.*

My brother warns me: *It's gonna get to be hell here for people like us. And lemme tell you something, you go somewhere else and say you're really Dominican, or whatever, and they won't give a shit. 'Cause you go to any other country, and you're just gonna be American to them.*

Inez, on the sofa, is rapt as she stares at the video images: a documentary on Afghanistan. The ruins of Kabul whiz by, recorded from a moving car. A woman, shot by a firing squad in a stadium, sinks beneath her burqa.

What the fuck is this? Is this propaganda, or something real?

On screen are three little girls, huddled in a corner as the reporter tries to talk to them. Three little girls, in a dirt-floored hut, with scarves pulled over their heads. None can talk. They are weeping.

It's propaganda and real – five days after the attacks.

Inez pulls the blanket around her head, weeps with the girls.

I glance out the window. I can see the buildings. I can see the towers there.

He hasn't come back.

The man who sobbed into his hands.

The fliers are still sitting there – the ones showing the shirtless man with dark eyes. They have been sitting there for two days.

Please help me find Andrew Fein.
He was on his way to a meeting at
MC Media in Tower 2, 86th Floor.
Andrew is 27 years old, 6' 2" and 180 lbs.
He had a leather portfolio with him.
Anyone who has any information please contact
me 718 555 2324

I'm taking these, I say when I leave at the end of the day.

I put the fliers in my backpack along with a roll of tape that's sitting on the counter. I walk west to St. Vincent's. Everywhere near the hospital entrance, there are fliers with pictures of the missing: they are on the wall on 11th Street, on the chain-link fence, even covering the front of Ray's Pizza, which is closed.

I walk back to the wall on 11th Street.

Among the flowers, the candles, the pleas for help, there is barely any space.

And then I see it. I see you.

Miriam Borcher
Born 1947
She works for Stanhope and Partners, One WTC
88th floor
She had polio as a child and has trouble walking.
She also has a speech impediment.
If you find her in a hospital, please call me at 917-
555-2243 (cell)
Please tell me where she is.

The picture is of the two of you together in a rowboat, on a lake, and in the background, red autumn leaves.

Had I seen this picture before? In your office once? On your desk?

This was who you used to go back to in Rye: short hair, glasses, sturdy.

You're both grinning into the camera.

Did she ever come to pick you up at work? It was the kind of office where your coworkers would ask about her by name but never acknowledge who she was. You were not exactly closeted, but you were not out either.

Was it any different at this next place, on the 88th floor of One WTC?

I look downtown. There is nothing where the Towers should be but smoke. There are no buildings.

Around me, young guys with backpacks squint to look at the fliers. Children place flowers at the base of the wall. Men in too tight jackets murmur prayers to saints.

I hear the footfall of boots. A group of National Guardsman have arrived. They're wearing fatigues, grimfaced, some blinking back tears.

'Soldiers!' a little girl calls out.

THE WORLD'S FAIR

God didn't make Flushing; it's all landfill. Ashes that the garbage men of Brooklyn dumped on Queens. Rats used to run all over. People who lived in shanties trapped animals here. My grandmother remembers this – watching trash torch and glow at night across a field. 'All of this,' she says, looking out at the garden apartments broken up by big brick buildings, 'it used to be garbage.'

'When did it stop being garbage?' I want to ask her.

'Before you were born,' she offers, 'this neighborhood was beautiful.'

As if my being born ruined it.

She's obsessed with this old movie theater on Northern Boulevard. 'You should have seen The Keith. It was a palace. You could see the lights from Main Street. The fountain in the lobby used to run.'

So we go up to The Keith, Tony and me, to see *Star Wars*. The fountain doesn't have anything in it but a dried layer of scuzz. The lobby smells like pee. I have to hold my breath to get to my seat. Tony buys a joint off this guy, and I swear it must be treated, because by the time R2-D2 comes out and starts squeaking and shit, I feel like I'm plugged into the wall.

'You feeling funny?' I ask Tony.

'Not funny enough,' he says.

'Naw, I mean funny bad.'

'Nuh... Aww... A little...' he finally says, so I know he's just making this up, so I'll feel okay.

The music gets all big and scary and Darth Vader shows up on the screen. A cardboard bucket suddenly shoots up and popcorn rains down on us. About five people scream at the same time, and then a bunch of guys start looking around the theater for who threw the popcorn.

'What, it's the *Rocky Horror* fucking *Picture Show* now?' Tony asks, tilting his head back.

'I don't feel well,' I tell him.

'What?' he asks, as if I'm speaking in code. 'You mean like you're gonna throw up?'

'I don't feel well,' I tell him again.

'You wanna go?'

The scary music is pounding. I think, maybe there really is something wrong with my chair. Maybe there's a broken wire under it, and I am getting electrocuted. Or the guy behind us, drinking his beer and slapping his knees whenever one of the little robots gets fucked up, rigged this thing up to electrocute me and Tony. If I tell Tony this, he'll think I'm crazy. But if I don't tell him, we both might die.

'I think the pot's treated,' I tell Tony finally. 'I think someone dusted it.'

'You okay?' he wants to know.

'No,' I tell him.

I can tell he doesn't wanna go. He picks up his leather jacket like he's a little kid who has to leave his friend's toys and come home.

'Stay,' I whisper. 'I'll come find you afterward.'

'Can you two shut up so the rest of us can hear the movie?' the knee-slapper behind us asks.

'You think it's a fucking library in here?' Tony asks, standing up. I pull him away from the guy and act like he's gonna be really threatening.

Tony used to get beat up every day after school until he cut his hair real short, got this leather jacket with zippers all over it, tore up his t-shirts, and started wearing Levi's with straight legs. He even learned how to break off the sharp end of a safety pin so that it looks like it's going through his cheek. People are scared to come too close to him, but there are some guys who drive down Northern sometimes and toss bottles at him, screaming 'Punk!'

Outside, the night air is waiting. But the electricity followed. I take a deep breath, and the charge weakens.

'Better?' Tony asks.

'A little,' I answer.

Cars whiz by, slap light in our faces.

We start to walk down Main Street, past the boarded

up stores. At night the avenue is so empty, every footstep seems to echo. Up ahead there's the store they torched, its ruins gaping like a mouth and its smell still hanging in the air a week after the fire. An airplane goes over us, its belly so shiny and big I think I can reach up to it with my hand. Its boom drowns everything out.

Tony's pouting, walks all hunched over, his hair making his shadow look like the shadow of a cartoon character. Once the plane passes, he starts to sing, 'I'll take Manhattan, the Bronx and Staten Island too...'

Tony's parents wanted him to be a singer, like Frank Sinatra or something, and every now and then one of those old songs pops out. But mostly he listens to the Sex Pistols and Patti Smith and The Clash. His parents think that spending time in the Village messed him up, and they're trying to keep us from going into the city anymore. 'It's the drugs!' his mother says, when she tries to explain what's bad about it.

We get near the subway station, and I think Tony's gonna say we should go to the Village, and I can't right now – not with this electricity going through me. And neither of us has any money, and we just spent everything he had on *Star Wars*.

'What do you want to do?' I ask.

Tony shrugs, his hands stuffed so deep down his pockets I think they'll come right through the front of his jeans.

I ask, 'Wanna go to the World's Fair?'

The World's Fair ended something like fourteen years ago. Tony and I were just kids then, so little that our parents had to push us around in baby carriages. My earliest memory is of the World's Fair. They had these strollers that looked like rocket ships, and you could rent them for a quarter. But my parents said it was dumb to pay a quarter for that, so I never got to ride in one. We went to Futurama and it was all about how cool cities would be when Tony and I grew up. There were supposed to be moving sidewalks, and flying cars, and synthetic food. I guess the only part that really came true was the synthetic food. And there was this scale model of the city, every building sitting there in miniature, all perfect and clean.

Now, the World's Fair doesn't have anything left except for some old rusty rocket ships and a see-through globe. But Tony and me, when we go there at night, the sky opens up, big and dark and stretching over us without any interruption. The lights there aren't like streetlights; they're like stage lights. We're the only ones there most of the time. Everybody leaves us alone.

'Hey,' I tell Tony. 'Let's go to my house. I'll get some money from my father, and we can buy some Remy Martin and take it to the World's Fair.'

My father's watching TV when we get there, an old war movie. That's good. When he's watching old war movies, he doesn't see anything else. If he's not watching a war movie, he's talking about the war. If he's not talking about the war, he's talking about all the houses he built. 'Half of Flushing,' he says, his eyes turning down at the lie. 'How can I leave?' he asks because everyone keeps telling us to move, tells us it's gonna get bad. 'Like Bed Stuy. Like the Bronx. Worse,' they say, before they pack up their houses and move out to the 'burbs. And my father sits and tells them all, 'How can I go? My wife died here. My Julie grew up here. And Eve,' he says, pointing to me as if I can't hear or speak, 'she still has to finish high school.'

I hate when they tell us to leave, like they're going someplace good and clean, and we're going to burn with the neighborhood if we stay.

Down in the basement, I undo the brick. Then I take out the metal box. It's incredible to me that my father thinks the lock on this thing means anything, that he doesn't realize you can jam a paper clip in it and pop the lid right open. Then again, it's incredible to me that he keeps his cash in a box in a basement, that he doesn't think about how banks are a little better than they were during the Depression.

I pull up eighteen quarters. Big amounts, he'll notice, but little amounts he'll think are just a miscount.

I push open the back door. Tony's waiting outside. We walk without talking, stop at a liquor store where we won't get proofed, buy a bottle of Remy Martin. Tony puts it in his jacket's inner pocket. He almost struts away from the store, and on the corner, we run into a new guy selling loose joints.

'C'mon,' I say, trying to pull Tony away.

'This dusted?' Tony asks, taking a look at the guy's baggy.

'Clean as the mountain air,' says the guy, blank eyes and

stringy hair. 'It's grown by elves in Vermont.' The guy doesn't have even a hint of a smile.

Tony takes four quarters from my pocket, drops them into the guy's hand, then takes the joint. Me, I still have a little bit of electricity chasing me.

The park where they put the World's Fair didn't have any houses on it at first because it was all mud – mud waves slapped apart anything people tried to build. Then they figured out how to drain the water into the river and made the ground solid. The park is three miles big. It is the geographic center of New York. The see-through globe, known as the unisphere, was a trademark of the fair and a symbol of hope and unity to people throughout the world. I had to memorise this stuff for school.

The park is completely empty when we get there. There's no water in the pool under the globe. The fountains haven't worked for years. There's graffiti all over the place – everyone's tagged it: SaneSmith, and Ghost, and Caine1, and Iz. Nearby, there's a building that looks like it was made out of giant toilet paper rolls. Then, near that, there're a couple of old rockets. I don't even know if these things are real or not. They could just be models. They're all rusty and shit. Tony walks over and makes his usual joke. 'Even I don't know if I'm gonna be able to get these things started again.'

He's the only one who calls me Even. I smile and give Tony a little punch on his shoulder. Then I take the bottle of Remy Martin from him.

He sings, 'God save the Queen. She ain't no human being.'

He tries to sound as pissed off as he can while he sings this and his lower lip curls. It's really cute.

We walk over to the see-through globe and we get right underneath it. There's a U-shaped swerve of steel holding it up, almost like a stand. The lights make everything look really weird – caught in the act, frozen.

'If you could go anywhere in the world,' I ask Tony, 'where would you go?'

Another plane flies over us, good and low from LaGuardia, threatening to drown everything with its sound. Tony grins and says something but with the plane on its way out, I can't hear.

'What?' I mouth.

'England,' he says.

Obvious. All his obsessions leading there, except for Patti Smith of course. She's from New Jersey.

'How about you?' Tony asks.

'Brazil,' I tell him, looking up at the globe.

Tony wants to know, 'How come?'

'Because it's way the fuck down here and if we climbed up we might be able to reach it.'

I try to pull myself up onto the stand and fall down again.

Tony laughs. 'Ya know, Rio is even worse than New York.'

I touch my knee, which hurts a little after the fall.

'Seriously,' Tony says. 'It's fucked up there. And we'd have to learn Portuguese. But London. That's a whole other story.'

He isn't smiling. He's serious.

I go over to him and take the Remy Martin and have a swig.

'We already know the language,' he says. 'And the whole thing's like a toy. Just look at those double decker buses and the way the cops dress.'

I think about this for a second, imagine shiny, red double decker buses small enough to move with my hand, a Piccadilly Circus I can fit on my basement floor.

'You still getting electrocuted?' Tony asks.

'No,' I tell him, savoring the calm, 'it's stopped.'

Tony takes the joint from his pocket and lights it up.

'There are squats all over London,' he says and takes another toke.

'What do you mean?'

'We could live for free.' He lets out a blob of smoke.

'We'd need passports,' I remind him.

'Then we'll get passports,' Tony says, taking another hit.

'We need to get our parents' permission.'

'We'd need to get their signatures,' Tony says. 'I can do their signatures.'

I go back over to the globe, shut my eyes and pretend its spotlights are sunlight.

'It rains all the time in England,' I say.

'I like rain.'

The song Tony was singing before comes into my head.

'There's no Queens in it,' I notice.

Tony asks, 'What?'

'It goes, "I'll take Manhattan, the Bronx and Staten Island too." There's no Queens in it.'

I take the joint from Tony while he thinks about this.

'There's no Brooklyn either,' he says.

'Staten Island,' I laugh, taking a hit. 'Who the fuck goes to Staten Island anyway?'

Another plane flies over us. We both turn our faces to the sky.

'I met this guy,' says Tony. 'In Washington Square Park. He's from London... I've got his address.'

I hand the joint back to Tony and lie down on the cold concrete of the dry pool. Tony takes a hit and comes and lies next to me. He hands the joint back.

'Even,' he says. 'I'm going. Will you come with me?'

I hold the smoke in my lungs, exhale, ask him, 'What are we gonna do when we get there?'

'Sing,' says Tony. 'Dance. Ride double decker busses.'

'Will we have tea with the Queen?' I ask, handing back the joint.

We both laugh.

Tony sings, 'God save the Queen. She ain't no human being.'

'So mean,' I chide.

'Yeah,' says Tony, as if resigned. 'We'll have tea with the Queen.'

He stubs out what's left of the joint.

'Even,' Tony asks, 'you gonna come with me so we can get our passports?'

The sky is crisscrossed with soaring planes. I put my hand on Tony's cold leather jacket to make sure he's there.

'Okay,' I tell him.

We're going to get out of this place. For real. One day they'll wake up. We won't be here. They'll wish we said goodbye, but they won't come after us. We'll be gone.

WAITING FOR DAYLIGHT

It's true I remember noon in Scretton as blinding – waking up groggy and hurting, squinting while I lifted the shade during the only time the sun was high in wintertime. The walk to McCusker's was all a blur. I always charged along the January sidewalks angry and fast, taking the wind against me personally. The snow was gray from the soot of car exhaust. The ice melted and reformed in slick, sharp puddles I accidentally walked into, soaking my sneakers with painfully cold runoff. In McCusker's, I welcomed the steamy windows and the smell of bacon fat. The other regulars nodded to me. Jimmy Sloane, the landlord and coke dealer who had gone to Scretton College and never left town, held court at one of the booths and regarded everyone else with the knowledge of a man who owned the town; Avery Todd, damp-haired and looking over her paper at the man damp-haired across from her too, a different one every time; and Louis Scott, who, like me, was just a little too strange to fit in at the college and took his coffee alone – they were all there.

This was what I had wanted: the most exotic thing I could imagine, a small town where everyone knew who you were, knew your shortcomings and kept talking to you, kept treating you like family anyway. I had chosen Scretton College based on the pictures in its catalogue – happy, slightly hippy looking students smiling before a torch-red background of New England leaves, leaning back against stone walls as they read, walking with friends across the town's covered bridge and then sitting ruddy-faced in the school's snackbar sipping cocoa after, I assumed, the earlier walk across the bridge. They looked clean and happy and loved, and, most of all, rich, and I wanted to be one of them.

Scretton College had chosen me based on my ability to con, or so I believed. They could not have chosen me based on my high school grades, because I had dropped out of high school, and, instead, after spending two years on the road and taking my GED, presented them with an essay outlining the best laundromats to sleep in between Albany and Cape Cod.

'Brilliant,' said Dale Curran, the school's academic dean, when I showed up for my campus interview. He asked me if I'd read any Jack Kerouac. I lied and said I had. He told me the school could come up with some scholarship money to make up the difference between my basic grant and student loan. Tuition at Scretton College cost more than anyone I knew made in a year. I looked around at the campus, the verdant, lush lawns then preening in the August air. I walked through the solid, stone dormitories, certain they would be warm and easy in winter. Students at Scretton College were all given private rooms – no sharing anything except cocaine in the bathroom between classes. I said I would be happy to attend Scretton College in the fall.

Very quickly I discovered that Scretton College needed me as much as I needed it. Scretton was where rich kids got sent when they fucked up too much to go anywhere else. At Scretton's tiny classes, I was one of the few students who showed up for lectures, and one of the fewer who spoke during seminars and wrote papers. I quickly began to draw more attention to myself than felt healthy, and, as a result, I needed to go to the pub at night in order to fit in, downing shots of tequila until everything but me and Avery Todd faded.

Avery was startlingly beautiful, tall and dark-haired, with eyes so devastatingly deep, no one could stare at them for too long – it was that dangerous. She wore heels that accentuated her height and red lipstick that made her large, laughing mouth seem positively elastic. 'Wouldn't wish someone here sober,' she would announce, after looking around the damp basement bar and before knocking back a V and T, what she'd taken to calling vodka and tonics.

'Damn straight,' I'd agree, downing another shot.

'Next time my daddy says it's Scretton or Siberia,' she continued, 'I'll take Siberia.'

Avery was from an oil rich Texas family who hadn't acted kindly when she'd taken to the Houston streets trying life under an assumed name to keep them back. She'd slipped into the arms of a lover who she spoke of constantly, but had never seen again after a nasty bust, during which the cops found her and her lover Michael with lines of liquid sky all cut to go. Michael, older than Avery, was somewhere doing time while Avery was let go after an in-patient detox stint and signed up at school. The judge said it was okay after Avery's father had slipped him five thousand dollars. Avery's parents stuck her in Scretton with no spare cash, fearing she'd spend it on drugs, and, as a result, Avery became a barfly hustler extraordinaire. 'Honey bear,' she said, sidling up to some shy preppy boy who wriggled beneath her touch. 'You getting something? Get me something too. I don't have any money. My father doesn't love me.'

'Jesus,' I said to Avery. 'What're you complaining about? He bought you a frigging judge.'

'This girl doesn't understand anything,' Avery explained to that evening's boy, as she gestured toward me. 'Just right out of New York City's gutters, isn't that right, hon?'

It was one of those stupid things that Avery only said when she was very drunk, so I figured the best thing to do was walk away. Then I walked right into Dale Curran, the academic dean at the college, who said to me, 'Hey, it's Mary Vega!'

'Hello,' I said.

I was not surprised to see him there. We were in the only bar in town.

'Mary, your professors are saying great things about you.'

'They are?' I asked. Unlike Avery, I did sometimes like the town's smallness. It forced people to cross lines that would normally be between someone like Dale and me. It forced everyone to live together.

Dale sat near the door like a father wanting to ask where each of his children was going, his prematurely gray hair hanging in damp bangs against his forehead, a man from the 1960s who wore his suit and his age awkwardly, as if he still could not believe either belonged to him. He had a trick eye that never focused like the other one, and as I watched his face now, I wondered whether one eye was glass.

'It's cold out there,' he said, motioning to the door with his head.

I smiled and shrugged.

'Whyn't you have a seat?'

I stared at the empty stool next to Dale. If I sat there, he would feel compelled to buy my drinks. Avery, usually, could manage to hustle drinks for both of us. 'Buy a drink for my friend too,' she would whisper, tracing her long, red nails against the broadcloth backed buttons of a man's shirt. And it almost always worked, as if she was buying for me by proxy, but now I was on my own. I sat.

'What can I get you?' Dale asked.

'Tequila sunrise,' I said, surprised to find my voice was a whisper.

'Well, well,' Dale laughed. 'Mary Vega. I remember when I could drink tequila all night. Who says that youth is wasted on the young?'

I smiled and lifted my drink when the bartender brought it, touching my glass to Dale's as he brought his to mine, downing half of it in a gulp and wishing the sweetness lasted longer than the bitterness.

'Aren't you going to take your coat off?' he asked.

'I'm cold,' I answered, unable to get my voice loud again.

'Ah yes,' Dale answered. 'Those damned New Hampshire winters. You can't get them out of your blood.'

I nodded.

'Something wrong?' he asked.

'No,' I answered. 'Nothing's wrong.'

'Just the winter blues then,' he said reassuringly. 'I get them too.'

I tried to smile, looked behind me, back where Avery was dancing with the awkward preppy boy, moving all over him like she was god and wind and the boy was just a lamppost. Avery never dressed like she was cold, came down to the bar dressed in a tight black t-shirt and light cotton skirt, leaving trails of patchouli to take over the stale beer air.

'Mary,' Dale said. 'I've been wanting to talk to you because I admire your sense of poetry, and there's so little to admire this time of year, so little poetry in this town. I used to write too, you know.'

'You did?' I asked.

'Now look at me. I'm just an administrator in a shit college town.'

It was funny to hear Dale use the word 'shit,' as if someone else had lent it to him, but he didn't own it. I was drunk enough so I even laughed a little. Dale looked disturbed, and I immediately felt a little bit bad, as if all I could do that night was hurt people, not badly but unintentionally, like someone who wasn't quite having the same conversation as everyone else.

'How do you like it?' he asked.

'Me? It's alright.'

He sneered.

'It's not bad.'

'Not bad,' he repeated. 'Not bad for who?'

'Me, I guess.'

'No,' he answered. 'It can't be good for you either. Look at what it's doing to you. You're turning into one of them.'

'What do you mean?' I asked.

'When you came here, you were loud and meaningful,' he said. Then hunting for something in the pocket of his sports jacket, and coming up with a packet of cigarettes, he continued, 'You had style, charisma.'

The word 'charisma' didn't work for him either. He said it like a man speaking a foreign language from a phrase book.

'And that great accent.'

'Accent?' I asked.

He laughed out the side of his mouth. 'People with accents never think they have accents.'

He switched the subject to William Carlos Williams, and Williams' love of immigrants. I was hungry to talk poetry. 'Where are your people from?' he slipped in.

'New York,' I answered.

He raised one eyebrow, the one over the eye that moved.

'My father's Cuban,' I said at last, giving him the answer he wanted.

'Do you speak Spanish?' he asked me.

'No,' I told him.

Then he veered again back to poetry. And we talked poetry during the rest of the night. And then the night began to snuff itself out. The boys who played lacrosse on the lawns left in a group, the girls who skied walked along in disappointment to a midnight clear without promise of snow, and finally Avery giggled as the boy in the broadcloth shirt followed. 'Goodnight,' she whispered, to both Dale and me, and as she went, I recognized that moment was my last hope, like a life preserver being pulled in so that only the gray of sea stretched in icy peaked waves.

The lights flickered for the final warning on last call.

'Can I give you a ride home?' Dale asked.

'Yes,' I said, when I heard Avery's steps end at the top of the flight of stairs.

We walked out into the dark parking lot, lit occasionally by cars pulling out. He fished in his pockets and came up with an empty packet of cigarettes.

'Do you mind?' he asked, showing me the empty packet. 'I have a carton in my office. Can we stop there first?'

Of course, I knew you were never supposed to agree to stopping off anywhere when you accepted a ride from a man. Everyone knew that. And my heart did a little roll and I wanted to say, no, it was not okay. But this was the vice president of the college, and he would certainly be insulted if I were to tell him I was going to walk home after all.

'Sure' I said to him

Had he seen my hesitation? Had I already ruined something in this small town where everyone gossiped about everyone else?

He led me to a beat up Volkswagen, and laughed as I was about to get in. 'Just kidding,' he said, then unlocked the door of the new BMW parked next to it.

We drove down the vacant streets to the administration building, the smell of cigarettes and leather seats thick in the air. 'Come in,' he said, when we arrived. 'I want to show you something.'

The administration building at night was frightening, enormous and gothic, and Dale did not turn the lights on. We felt our way to his office with hands against the wall, squinting in the dim shadows lit by the single streetlight from the main street. When we arrived in his office and he flicked the switch, the light was blinding, and I stood for a minute letting my eyes adjust. Avery was in the warm cave of her room with the boy, showing him what she called her womb room, the tapestries softening the hard walls. She'd slip her shirt off giggling, undo the skirt, fall with him on the feather eiderdown her mother had ordered for her from Germany. She'd light the candles she wasn't supposed to have in her room, put on an old Billie Holliday album, humming with Lady Day. Avery, one big fire hazard.

My eyes focused on the skull Dale kept on a shelf. He took it down, showed it to me, his pale, awkward hands more awkward with drunkenness. He said something about a romantic poet thrown out of college for drinking from a skull. Then the room began to move slightly, like an image in a slide projector the projectionist has not found the right height for, slipping then stopping, again and again.

'Sit,' said Dale. 'You look dizzy.'

I sat in the leather seat across from the couch far from his desk. He placed the skull back on the shelf.

'They were all cut off from the others,' he said. 'Byron for being a madman and H.D. for being a lesbian.'

I nodded as if I knew what he was talking about.

'Are you a lesbian?' he asked.

I stared at him.

'Avery,' he threw in. 'You're in love with her, aren't you?'

And if anyone, if anyone else at all, would have said that to me, then I might have said, yes, that's true. But instead, Dale Curran asked, like a threat, so I told him, 'We're friends.'

'Of course,' he told me.

He went to the desk, pulled a carton of cigarettes from a drawer, took a packet out, tapped the packet against the desk and opened it. He lit one with the lighter he pulled from his pocket, then sat on the couch across from me. 'This is as good a time as any,' he said, 'to let you know that there's one dean's scholarship to give out for next year, and I want to see to it that you're the one who has it.'

'Thank you,' I whispered.

'I know you can't keep coming here without it.'

He looked at his cigarette for a moment, as if it would provide him with the next thing he needed to know.

'Mary,' he said, continuing the transfixion with what burned. 'Tell me how you feel about this college.'

'I like it,' I told him quickly.

'Tell me how you feel about me.'

I looked outside, wishing it was light already, wishing it was high noon, wishing I was walking into McCusker's hungover and wanting coffee, and seeing everyone I knew – Jimmy Sloane rubbing his nose, Louis Scott lonely, and, most of all, Avery Todd rubbing her red-nailed fingertips against the moisture on the window, drawing a space that she could look out, so she would see the world through condensation. And while I was thinking this, I felt Dale's hand come near me, and I ignored it at first, because I knew what was happening should not have been happening, so I ignored it, but then his hand was very close to my chest, and, automatically, my hand shot up to stop his.

He shook my hand off.

'Carol Lynley,' he said, 'was a movie star who used to play street kids who thought they knew everything, but she looked so innocent, nothing could touch her. Nothing can touch you, Mary.'

He reached for my chest again, and again, I tried to stop him, and again, he shook me off, harder this time. Then he had his hand down the front of my shirt and he said to me – He said, 'You really don't get it, do you?'

THE YOUNG WOMAN
SLEEPS WHILE THE
ARTIST PAINTS HER

The young woman sleeps while the artist paints her.

She was up late, fighting with her boyfriend. Her boyfriend told her she was selfish, wasn't looking after his needs. He wanted to sleep with other women. He wanted her to be open, generous.

The young woman sleeps while the artist paints her.

The artist is one of the instructors at the college, and the artist asked the young woman if she would sit for a portrait. The artist has short blond hair, a snub nose, a hushed voice. Many of the students complain about the artist. She doesn't tell them what they should do to make their work better. She doesn't talk to them enough at all. The college is a private one, and the other students complain a lot. But the young woman likes the artist. When she and the artist are alone, the artist says a lot.

She tells the young woman about going to Europe for the first time. She tells her about seeing all the paintings that she has only seen reproductions of before. She tells her how disappointing it was to see some of the originals; the slides she had seen of those paintings in art history class seemed more vivid than the paintings themselves. The colors were more intense when images of the paintings were projected onto a screen; the masterpieces seemed to glow and were imbued with light. The real paintings were smaller, more subdued, and you had to dodge around the other visitors to even glimpse them.

The young woman has three jobs this semester: she works in the college bookstore, and she poses nude for life drawing classes, and now she is modelling for the artist.

The young woman is not naked in the painting that the artist paints. Her shoulders are bare, but she is covered by a sheet. She lies on a cot with a small pillow under her head. All the linen matches. It is white cotton with a blue check. The young woman is pleased that, in the portrait, she is depicted sleeping. She closes her eyes while she and the artist speak to one another. Sometimes the artist focuses only on painting and does not speak. Sometimes the young woman really does fall asleep.

The young woman sleeps while the artist paints her.

When she models for life drawing classes, she has to sit naked on a platform in a big room. The art classes are held in a converted barn, where it's always cold A space heater is nearby to keep her warm. By the time the class is underway during the winter months, it is already dark outside. Sometimes she watches snow fall on the small town streets while she poses. There are twenty people in the class, all her age, all drawing her. She holds still. She hates to hold still. But sitting there, naked, pays twice as much as the other student jobs, and she needs time to study.

Every now and then, something will happen that makes the young woman realize she cannot leave the life drawing class alone. She'll put on her bathrobe and rush to a male friend in the class and ask him, Will you walk me home? And, after a while, he will simply offer. He will wait while she dresses. Sometimes he and a female friend will wait too, and they will all walk back to her house together. Years later, she will not be able to tell you what triggered the fear. But she knows the other life drawing models – who are all young women – also ask male friends in the class to accompany them during the walk home. None of the male friends have any trouble understanding the purpose of their company following a drawing session.

The young woman sleeps while the artist paints her.

At the start of every semester, the college's business manager approaches the young woman, and she tells the young woman she has added up the grants, and work study funds, and low interest student loans available to the young woman. And she tells the young woman: I don't think you can afford to study here. And the young woman takes the papers from the business manager, and she tells her, I'll get another job.

The young woman sleeps while the artist paints her.

The young woman has also been to Europe; she went there because she won something called the Exceptional Overseas Scholarship. She had not seen any slides of masterpieces before she went, but the *Mona Lisa* did seem small to her and she wished it had not been behind bulletproof glass. She sat in cafes drinking white wine after class, and she ate sandwiches made out of stuffed grape leaves and baguettes, and she sat in front of the Centre Pompidou watching the skateboarders and talking to her friends.

The young woman discloses that she hates this place, wants to leave, is only here because she is so close to finishing that it doesn't make sense to leave now. The artist agrees that it is hard to go back to a place when you've been somewhere else that you love. The artist says, being in a new place changes you and you're never the same person again. The artist tells the young woman about a movie that's just come out: it's about an Australian reporter in Indonesia. And this movie, the artist says, shows how the reporter changes when he is in Indonesia. She thinks the young woman would enjoy seeing this movie.

The young woman sleeps while the artist paints her.

When the artist first asked her to sit, she thought *good*, because the artist was a woman, and there would be no risk, no subtext, no misunderstanding. The young woman saw other paintings in the studio, and she realized some were of the artist's husband. I like faces like this, the artist said. And when the young woman saw the husband's nose, and the contours of his face, she thought, the artist likes Jewish faces; she wants to paint me because I am Jewish. She wondered what she would look like in the painting. Would she look the way she imagined she looked? Would her nose look longer?

The young woman sleeps while the artist paints her.

The artist stops speaking, and the young woman almost drifts off, and while she does, she remembers being introduced to the very famous poet. The young woman arrived for the very famous poet's reading early. No one but her writing instructor and the very famous poet were there. 'This is the young woman I was telling you about,' the writing instructor said to the very famous poet. The very famous poet smiled at her. 'And this,' the writing instructor said to her, 'is the very famous poet.' He had long hair, and a beard, and was short and elfin. He looked just like all the pictures she'd seen of him.

'Hello,' she said.

'I'm glad to meet you,' the very famous poet said back.

'Will you get us some coffee?' the writing instructor asked.

The young woman took their coffee orders and went to the snack bar to get their coffee. She brought it back. This young woman is one of the best students I've ever had, the writing instructor said. And he shifted his chair, ready to include her in conversation with the very famous poet. But the young woman was tired. She'd had another fight with her boyfriend the night before. She left the poets and returned to her seat in the audience.

The young woman sleeps while the artist paints her.

As she drifts off, she wallows in regret. She loved the very famous poet's work. In fact, his poems were the first ones she'd committed to memory. She felt as if he was writing about a world she knew. He and the writing instructor were young poets together. They'd lived in New York then, loved its unpredictability, dropped acid and drank until the writing instructor couldn't drink anymore and had to go dry before he moved to New England. She was also from New York, and while she couldn't remember the version of the city the very famous poet and the writing instructor wrote about, she understood their celebration of its chaotic streets. Those were streets she knew. And she thinks that she does not belong here, in rural New England. She is bothered by the silence of the streets, the snow blanketing the hills, the smoke curlicuing up from the chimneys on the houses. It is all very eerie to her. She hates the bitter winter wind, the banks of snow that block driveways and paths, and the opaque plastic taped over the windows to shut out the drafts.

The young woman sleeps while the artist paints her.

At the end of the session that day, the artist tells the young woman she is done. The artist says she will continue to work on the painting, but she does not need a model anymore. The artist takes out a roll of bills and gives the young woman an extra fifty. She tells the young woman to stop by later in the year. She says the painting will be ready to show then.

The young woman is standing on a subway train years later, holding onto a pole because there aren't any seats.

The train is roaring and, in the dark tunnel, the windows of the train will become reflective, and she'll see a faint image of herself looking back at her. It will almost look as if it was painted and then, the memory will return to her – of posing for the painting that the artist did.

The young woman appreciates the anonymity of the city every day, happily watches people on the streets she doesn't know. And, more importantly, is pleased that they do not know her.

The young woman never returned to the small town again, with one exception – she went back for the writing instructor's memorial service after he died of lung cancer.

The boyfriend had to be broken up with again and again. Every time they ended it, he reappeared, begging for her forgiveness.

When she remembers her years in the small town, she remembers exhaustion, never being able to fully focus on work, never being able to fully focus on studies. She remembers the cough she couldn't shake.

And she remembers the painting. She remembers going back to the artist's house, and trying to be patient when the artist made her a cup of herb tea. She should not rush to see the painting, she realised. After all, many people did not like portraits of themselves. They did not think that the portraits looked like them. She and the artist had discussed this. Many people found paintings of themselves unflattering.

Remember, the artist said, this is just an image of what I saw.

They picked up their cups of tea. They walked from the kitchen into the studio.

The young woman looked up, and she saw the painting, and she gasped at the sight of it.

The artist smiled at this.

The young woman in the painting was asleep, resting her head on the blue checked white linen. Her wavy blond hair was swept back. Light burnished her brow and cheeks. Her mouth was slightly open, and her nose was prominent.

It was the oddest thing, to be outside of herself like this, the young woman thought, completely different to a photo, seeing yourself as someone else's construction.

It was her. It was not her.

THE CHRISTMAS STORY

The studio was dark and cold when I arrived. Snow covered all the skylights. It had taken me twice as long as usual to walk there, slipping and sliding along the way. I turned the heat up high, higher than I was supposed to. And I turned on the space heater near my desk. There was a slew of email messages I didn't want to answer: a reminder from the 5 Colleges Literature and Politics Consortium (5CLAP) that as writer-in-residence I was expected to do another community event during the year, a request from the *Valley Advocate* for an interview about the Truth and Reconciliation Commission book, an invitation to the 5CLAP year end holiday party.

And then I started to write what you asked me to write: a story for your daughters, for Rosa and Emma. Because they cannot read anything of mine that's published, I said, okay, I'll write them a Christmas story.

Snow never stayed on the ground in New York. Almost as soon as it fell from the sky, it was battered by traffic, stomped by booted feet. There were grimy dark snowbanks by the curb, and pools of slush everywhere else. The only place where you could find a real stretch of white snow was in the park, behind the playground. We'd go there with our metal-bladed Flexible Flyers, slide down the hill on our bellies, scream to warn the other kids as we careened out of control.

Leah Loggins lived by the entrance to the park, on Fort Washington Avenue. She had wavy blond hair that her mother braided before she went to bed each night and wore denim bib overalls and cotton peasant blouses. I wore the polyester polo shirts and pull-on bell bottoms that everyone else in the neighborhood wore. Teachers told me to brush my mud-colored hair even when I'd just brushed it. Leah lived on the west side of Broadway. We lived east.

'People in your neighborhood practice voodoo,' she said.

'No one practices voodoo,' I told her.

'There are dead pigeons where you live. It's for voodoo. Santería.'

'No it's not!'

Leah's apartment was unlike any place else I'd seen in the neighborhood Everything was in a neutral color. It was uncluttered, without carpeting or linoleum even. Sun speckled the wood floor in the living room.

Leah's mother, who we both called Vera, came in. She had shoulder-length gray-blond hair, and she always wore the same Indian cotton caftan. 'Why don't you girls string some popcorn for the tree?' she asked.

The Christmas tree was wide and bushy and so tall that it almost touched the ceiling.

'Do you always have a tree?' I asked. 'My mom won't get one because we're Jewish.'

'We are too,' Leah said.

'You are?'

Leah nodded. She was expertly stringing popcorn. My popcorn kept breaking into crumbs around the thread.

'Try the cranberries,' she advised.

They slid on the needle more easily but stained my fingers red.

'You should ask Jerry to get you a Christmas tree,' said Leah. 'He's not Jewish.'

Jerry was my mother's boyfriend. He moved in with her after she and my father divorced.

Lissy, Leah's little sister, entered the room. She was only two years old, and persistently booby-trapped the apartment with puddles of baby pee when she went diaperless. She was carrying a plastic dinner plate with her as she wandered around. I made a mental note not to use it.

'One time my daddy got really mad and threw our Christmas tree out the window,' Leah announced.

'Leah!' Vera pleaded. 'Don't tell people that.'

'I thought it was funny,' Leah said, pulling thread through a few more pieces of popcorn.

That night, I explained to my mother that I had helped decorate Leah's Christmas tree and I wanted one too.

'Hannah, we've been through this a million times. We're not getting a Christmas tree. We're Jewish.'

'Leah's Jewish,' I reminded her.

'Leah's father's isn't Jewish.'

'Jerry's not Jewish.'

'I am,' my mother said. 'And you are. And we're not getting a Christmas tree.'

You've asked me to explain this to you, asked: 'If you weren't religious, why couldn't you have a Christmas tree?'

Being Jewish culturally isn't the same as being religious, I explained.

Why, you wanted to know, didn't we have Chanukah then?

And, already that month, I'd had to explain over and over to well meaning-people wanting to wish me the right thing, no, Chanukah isn't Jewish Christmas. Even if you are religious, it isn't a very important holiday. It's just hyped up because of Christmas.

We were sitting in the snack room at the Chestnut Mountain Christmas Tree Farm, the scent of pine needles so powerful, it was as if we'd climbed inside a box of air fresheners. Pine mixed with the scent of sugar cookies and cloves. We were at a picnic table drinking our complimentary mugs of mulled cider. There were carollers from the Unitarian Church raising money for a women's education project in Guatemala, sometimes getting attention, sometimes being ignored, shutting their eyes as they sang. So earnest.

Sometimes tearful children ran in, seeking refuge from bullies in the crafts room, holding their damaged hand-made Christmas decorations.

Rosa appeared and announced she was bored, standing there in her big black sweater and black leggings. Emma followed, holding up a cardboard star covered with glitter.

The two trees we'd bought were already tied to the roof of your Volvo. One was for your house and the other was going to be dropped off with Emma and Rosa at their mother's.

I told you – didn't I – how odd I found it to be driving those roads with you, with those two Christmas trees and Sinead O'Connor singing 'Silent Night' on the radio? I told you – didn't I – that I didn't mind when Rosa and Emma did their sugared-up Sinead O'Connor imitations, didn't mind their whacky questions, didn't mind their direct pronouncements? Did I tell you that even though the weekends with them make me happy, take me away from the more brutal events I am writing about, I am always a little bit relieved when their weekends with us are over? I always exhale a little bit after we bring them to their mother's house, drop them off, drive away again.

I saw the little white dresses and veils in the shop window on upper Broadway. 'Mommy!' I called out. I wanted to know why they made little wedding dresses.

'Those are Communion dresses,' my mother answered. She pulled me past them and explained: 'They're for Catholics.'

I once overheard a teacher describing my mother as 'harried.' Her hair was always a mess, her lipstick never on straight. Her clothes – from years before – were too small and she rarely bought new ones. But now that she'd gotten my father to move out and was living with Jerry, she seemed more alive than ever before. Some sort of fear had left her.

My mother and Jerry were at their best when they were angry together, focusing on the same transgression. For example, often they were not acknowledged as a couple. Jerry was younger than my mother, and black, and when they went to restaurants, the host would try to seat my mother with just me. My mother's eyes would glow incandescent with outrage, and Jerry would take my mother's hand, and then we would all be seated at the same table, with my mother and Jerry expressing annoyance at the staff throughout the meal.

At home, they argued with abandon. They conspired by egging one another on. I remember, Jerry, who was always wearing his military surplus jacket, leaning back in the kitchen chair, arguing with my mother when he wanted to take on a political cause, and she would try to tell him to choose his battles. Deep acne scars pitted his face. I was not yet old enough to think of them as ugly; I thought they made his face interesting.

'We need a tenants' association,' Jerry announced.

The heat kept going off. We'd have it for a day or two and then, when we least expected it, wake up to face-slappingly freezing air. And when my mother turned the water on, I would hear her gasp become a gulp of despair, and I knew what it meant: there was no hot water.

We all had our jackets on all the time.

My mother stared at him for a second, then proceeded to put servings of Hamburger Helper onto our plates.

'Tenants' association, schmenants' association,' she said.

Jerry half-laughed.

I hated having to wear my coat all the time, the thick, mustard-colored wool made me feel as if I could never move the way a person should. And I dreaded the cold water I had to splash my face with in the morning. We heated bath water on the stove, but never got a tubful – just a few inches of water that got dirty and cooled off fast. In the afternoons, when I got home from school and Jerry and my mother weren't home yet, I wasn't allowed even to light the oven. My mother was terrified that the pilot would go out and the apartment would fill with gas. Sometimes when she'd light the oven at night, the flame would catch with a burst that left her scurrying back – the danger of our kitchen.

We could huddle in the kitchen with the gas stove on, but even then the kitchen was not really warm enough to be in jacketless.

'Okay,' she said. 'Let's go down to Florida and we'll talk to the landlord.'

Jerry started to smile.

'For real,' he said, 'someone's got to organize people.'
'You organize people.' She sat down. 'I'm through with it.'

The next day Jerry took me to the WBAI office to help print fliers. I turned the crank on the mimeograph, watching the wheel turn as the paper came out with what Jerry had written. I knew I had to turn the crank carefully, or the ink on the fliers would be uneven. Those fliers were perfect.

NEIGHBORS!!!
THERE IS SOMETHING WE CAN DO ABOUT:
NO HEAT OR HOT WATER
ROBBERIES IN OUR BUILDING
DIRTY ELEVATORS AND STAIRS
UNLOCKED LOBBY DOORS

There was also a Spanish translation of the fliers that Luisa Nieves wrote. She lived down the hall from us, and I used to get scared when I saw her coming down. She took crap from no one. Until I was fourteen, when I reached her height – five feet, four inches – I believed she was the biggest woman in the world. She was constantly in motion, grabbing her kids, especially skinny Roberto.

Roberto and I slid fliers under each apartment door, and we finished so fast, Luisa gave us some Chupa Chups. We sucked on them while we walked up and down the stairs. In a corner, near the staircase on the second floor, I found some comic books. They were just three panels long and a panel high. The characters in them looked like something from *Mad* magazine, but they all had problems – they had debt, or they'd committed a crime, or they were sick and were going to die. But they would meet someone who told them about Jesus, and no matter how hard things were, no matter much money they owed, or how many robberies they'd committed, or how sick they felt, they could accept Jesus into their hearts and enter His Eternal Kingdom.

I didn't know what an Eternal Kingdom was, but in the comic book it looked a lot like heaven, with angels and a bearded robed man reading from a book that shone light on his face. At the end of these comic books, the main character would always die, and either he would have accepted Jesus into his heart and gone to the Eternal Kingdom, or he would not have accepted Jesus and he'd face eternal damnation, which I knew was the worst thing that could happen. There was even a cartoon about a Jewish man, a Holocaust survivor, and he went to the Eternal Kingdom because he had the foresight to accept Jesus into his heart.

I didn't know how to accept Jesus into my heart. What did that mean? I said, 'Jesus, I accept you into my heart,' very softly at night, so that no one would hear me. I whispered, 'Jesus, I love you,' into my pillow before I went to sleep. I hoped that would be enough to save me from eternal damnation.

When I get back to your house in the evening, you're cooking dinner in your big gleaming kitchen with the island in the middle. The radio is on, so loud you don't hear me at first, and then you see me and come over to me wordlessly. The announcer's pompous pausing doesn't bother you; it bothers me. The announcer's contrived outrage about 'violence in our urban areas' doesn't bother you; it bothers me. The announcer's clumsy celebration of a new R & B group doesn't bother you; it bothers me. He's asking us to listen to the lyrics. He wants us to understand that the song isn't about sex; it's a young man singing that when he falls in love, it will be with a friend! He sounds as if he is amazed this is possible.

Everybody here means well. And that radio station – the one you listen to when you're cooking dinner – is like a distillation of meaning well. Everyone here simultaneously feels they deserve and don't deserve their upper middle-class lives. Everyone here is trying to figure out how to talk to and understand people and places that are not like the ones they know. Everyone here is white.

You tell me there are other people here from cities, international students, faculty from all over the world, exiles, refugees. And that's true, except that none of these people are considered the norm. You're the norm. I look like the norm. And the thing I find most painful isn't sticking out (because in their eyes, I don't), it's their assumptions that I'm one of them. It's that, when I tell them where I'm from they conclude, oh, it's really nice there, isn't it? It's that, where I came from, who I was before I came here, has been erased.

Your big, comfortable house smells like sautéed mushrooms and butter and the big bristly Christmas tree. And you wake me up when I have nightmares about the TRC stories, the victims' testimony, the assassins' confessions.

Someone looking in will see us sitting on the sofa with our glasses of wine and think how happy we look at home.

'What's a brothel?' I asked my mother.

I was setting the table in the kitchen. The windows were completely steamed up from the boiling spaghetti water.

'It's where prostitutes work,' my mother said. 'Why?'

'Is there a brothel on the fifth floor?'

'Yes,' she said. 'There is. Hannah, put the strainer in the sink for me.'

'Why is having a brothel here bad?' I asked my mother.

She looked surprised at first, rested the pot on the edge of the ceramic sink as the steam flew up in her face and made her sweat. Then, after a beat, she explained: 'It brings in a lot of strangers who don't belong here. It brings bad people in.'

'This guy told Jerry that the johns pee in the elevator.'

There was silence for a beat. Then my mother explained, 'The johns are the customers. They don't care about people who live here. If you see someone like that, stay away from them. Okay?'

I shrugged and drew Charlie Brown in the condensation, his round, bland face and his squiggle of forehead-pasted hair.

There was a second meeting in the lobby that Sunday. It went on all afternoon long. The grownups talked about building codes and tenants' patrols and rent strikes. Everyone who walked in was greeted by Jerry and Luisa. If we knew them because they lived there, they were spoken to warmly and invited to join in. There were also men on their own who came up to the building from the street, saw the meeting through the glass door, and walked away again. Roberto and I got bored, so we decided to race by running up one staircase, then across the lobby and up another staircase again, until Luisa pulled us aside and told us to play more quietly.

Instead, I decided to go upstairs, where my mother was sitting in the kitchen, with the stove on, reading *History Will Absolve Me* by Fidel Castro.

'How come you're not downstairs?' I asked.

'Because I'm not going to these meetings,' my mother said.

'Why not?'

'Because I'm tired.'

She had rings around her eyes and her hair was mussed and dry.

'Are we gonna have to have a picket line?' I asked her.

'Who said that?'

'They were talking about a rent strike downstairs.'

'A rent strike is where you don't pay your rent for a while. Until the landlord fixes things. It's not a picket line.'

'If we have a rent strike, we'll have more money, won't we?'

'You don't get to keep your money when you have a rent strike. You have to put it into escrow.' She saw my bewilderment and added, 'It's a special bank account. You keep your money there until the landlord fixes things. And a rent strike is the last resort. You have to try everything else first.'

She stared out the window then.

'Maybe we could go to Cuba one day,' she said. 'They have free medical care and it's hot there.'

I fell asleep before Jerry came home, and when I woke up, the air was frigid. Light seeped under the door. Jerry and my mother were in the kitchen. I could hear water running, and Jerry pleading: 'No!'

'I'm trying to help,' my mother said.

'It hurts,' Jerry explained with a gasp.

The walls were damp with condensation, weeping, clammy. I stood up, felt my way out of the room, found the light switch. When I reached the kitchen, I saw my mother trying to put a dishtowel against Jerry's face.

'Call the cops,' she said.

'No,' he answered. His face was swollen, a bruise darkening under his eye.

'Did the pimp do that?' I asked.

'Go back to bed,' my mother ordered

The next morning light, Jerry huddled in a corner of the kitchen while my mother made coffee. His bruise was even darker.

'Couldn't you call someone at *The Voice*?' my mother asked. 'Don't you have that friend at *The News*?'

'A slum in north Manhattan isn't a story,' Jerry said.

'Maybe you should make it one,' my mother advised.

So he and Luisa came up with a plan: banners painted inexpertly onto old bedsheets.

The first read:

MERRY CHRISTMAS! OUR CHILDREN DO NOT
HAVE ANY HEAT!

The second declared:

LANDLORD = SLUMLORD

The third one announced:

RENT STRIKE!

The banners flapped against the hard, dirty brick. They were supposed to shame our landlord, but they also shamed us. We were the people unfortunate enough to live there. 'You make us look bad!' an old man screamed at Jerry on the street. He actually flailed his hands in frustration. The Super told Luisa the banners had to come down, but she gave him one of her looks and walked away. And then The *New York Daily News* ran a story. They had pictures of the banners, a picture of Luisa and her children. And, finally, there was a picture of a beach with an empty deckchair facing the water. This, said the caption, was Miami Beach, where the building's landlord lived and he could not be reached for comment.

The next day, Jerry got a phone call. It was the landlord's management company. The landlord would like to inspect the building, they said. The landlord would also like to meet the tenants' committee. Could Jerry organize this?

Jerry was so happy, he went out and got me a bicycle. It had a banana seat, streamers, training wheels. 'Happy Chanukah!' he said.

'Happy Chanukah!' I said back.

I was pretty sure Chanukah was already over.

I rode the bike down to St. Nicholas Avenue, and back, and down to St. Nicholas Avenue and back. Roberto ran after me and asked for a chance to ride. Then I rode the bike over to the park and Leah came down with Vera and Lissy. She brought her bike, which didn't have any training wheels at all.

We raced around, laughing. Then Vera watched our bikes so we could go play on the rocks. She didn't realize we were planning to go to the Danger Caves. We walked along the top of the stone wall on Haven Avenue. We had to edge sideways and face New Jersey and the Hudson River, and then we would get to the rock caves which had once seemed huge, but now, as Leah and I were getting older, seemed much smaller. We couldn't stand in them anymore, but we could crouch down inside, and in the Danger Caves, amidst the condoms and broken glass, I found it: a crucifix.

The crucifix was made of pewter and was on a broken chain. I picked it up and wiped it against my pants.

'That has germs on it,' Leah said. 'You better clean it.'

When I got home, I washed the crucifix in soap and water and I put it underneath my pillow. 'I love you, Jesus,' I said to it, silently, at night, as I prayed for heat.

I kept the crucifix in my pocket and rubbed the contours of its surface whenever I needed reassurance. I told the crucifix, 'I accept you into my heart.'

You're going back to work? you asked, when I got ready to go back to the studio after dinner.

I reminded you I was working on *The Christmas Story*.

Walking through the town at night, if I looked into all the lovely homes with their Christmas trees I could believe I'd spirited myself into the world I wanted to live in as a child.

There are no fewer than five bookstores in this two-street town. The copy shop is run by a collective. You once saw James Baldwin sitting at the window table at Judy's. The town's population swells when the colleges are in session, to more than 35,000 people. I get to do an event at each institution involved in the Five Colleges Consortium – with the buttoned-up students of Amherst College, the privileged hippies of Hampshire, the serious young women of Smith, the isolated feminists of Mt. Holyoke and, most happily, with the chaotic crowds at the state university. A free bus system takes all the students from place to place, keeps their cars off the roads when they're drinking. Almost every musician touring the northeast stops here and plays the Mullins Center, or the Iron Horse, or Academy of Music.

It was the kind of place everyone wanted to live, wasn't it?

People called this – half-jokingly – the Happy Valley.

A blast of warm air hit me when I opened the door to the studio. I'd forgotten to turn the heat off. The snow on the skylight had melted and the room was bathed in moonlight. There was an enormous desk on trestles, a Herman Miller desk chair, a tan sofa and a glass coffee table and, off to the side, a small bedroom. My place for the year I am writer-in-residence.

If you had not come into my life during my first week in town, this is where I would sleep at night.

Two days before Christmas, the landlord came, and as he arrived, a photographer from *The Daily News* arrived also.

Jerry hadn't contacted *The News* about this. So who had? The landlord?

The landlord looked different than I thought he would. He was short and fat. And he was old, older than my father even. He wore a wool coat and was darkly tanned, like someone who spent every day on the beach. New York was freezing, gray. Luisa had sent Roberto to ring everyone's bells and tell them, 'The landlord's here. The landlord's here.' And then we all came out. We surrounded him. People began to shout things all at once. The Super stood by the landlord and folded his arms across his chest.

Someone shouted at the Super, 'What are you, his mamaguevo bodyguard, you fucking gusano?'

'Alright, simmer down. Simmer down,' the landlord said. 'I've come to tell you the boiler will be fixed.'

'When?' someone asked.

The landlord said: 'Today.'

A flashbulb went off. A reporter scribbled on his pads.

'I was unaware that there had been any problem—'

Luisa spat something under her breath that I couldn't understand.

'I was unaware,' he continued, like an exasperated father, 'there were problems here. Now, of course I have an investment in this property, and I'll do my best to rectify the situation. I'd like to meet with some of you to see how we can work together. Let's set up a time to talk some more. For now, I want to wish all of you a merry Christmas.'

And then, then he reached for a plastic garbage sack, and he started to pull out toys. A very little girl took a doll and a boy behind her took a truck. The landlord held up another doll and smiled. Everyone was silent for a moment. Then another little girl came and accepted it. The girls got dolls, and the boys got model cars. Luisa clung to Roberto, and my mother kept her hands on my shoulders. The landlord searched the crowd with his eyes, smiling creepily at the kids. And then his gaze alighted on me. I turned away and looked at the plastic car the boy held. The landlord noticed and asked, 'This?' He had dropped the doll back in the bag and was holding one of the model cars. My whole body tightened. I wanted that car. But my mother kept her hands firmly on my shoulders.

'No,' my mother said to the landlord.

And after that, nobody took any more toys.

The landlord shrugged. He followed the Super into the pee-smelling elevator. He rode upstairs and back down again. He walked from one end of the dirt-caked lobby to the other.

'Obviously the management firm I have hired hasn't been doing their job,' he announced. 'I'll figure it out after the holidays. For now, Merry Christmas! Happy Chanukah!'

And then, just before he went out the door, he muttered: 'You people live like pigs.' He glanced at my mother when he said this.

And then he was gone, swept off in the chocolate brown Cadillac that had been double-parked on the street.

That night, the heat came back on. We threw off our coats. We took hot baths and I stayed in the tub until my fingers wrinkled.

I washed the crucifix with soap and hot water.

We had a full day with heat, and then another day with heat, and then one more day until, on Christmas night, the radiators went cold again. There was no heat or hot water.

'Put your coat on,' my mother said.

She lit the oven in the kitchen.

'I hope there's a special hell for landlords.' She was trying to sound angry, but her voice almost caught in a sob.

A few hours later, the blue lights of police cars and ambulances bounced off the walls of the apartment and the brick of the building across the street. Jerry ran downstairs to find out what was happening.

'They found the family upstairs unconscious,' Jerry explained when he came back. ' All of them. The cops think they turned on the oven to heat the place and they must have fallen asleep. The flame must have gone out.'

My mother's eyes became enormous. Her brow tightened. This was one of the things she had warned me about – the gas seeping out when there was no flame anymore, the apartment filling with gas while we slept. She knew people did this to heat their apartments when the boiler broke down, and she did too, but she always did so fearfully.

'I'm going down to the hospital,' Jerry said.

'For God's sake,' my mother cried out. 'What can you do there?'

'I can tell people about it,' he said, getting his tape deck. Then he said to my mother: 'Call Danny and see if he can get someone there from *The Voice*.'

'Can I come with you?' I asked Jerry.

He was about to say yes, but my mother looked at him.

'The hospital will be warm,' Jerry said to her.

My mother hesitated, then said, 'Alright.'

I scrambled down the steps with Jerry. There were two cop cars outside and an ambulance. A small crowd was gathering, some of them people we knew. Jerry nodded hello to them all. The back of the ambulance was open; the driver stood waiting. Jerry walked over and introduced himself. 'C'I talk to you?'

'You family?'

'I live here,' Jerry said. 'I'm on the tenants' committee.'

The driver looked away from him, looked straight ahead.

'You going down to Columbia Presbyterian?' Jerry asked.

Columbia Presbyterian was the nearest hospital.

The driver shook his head. He said, 'We're going to Sydenham.'

Sydenham was all the way down in Harlem.

'Columbia Pres is a zoo,' the driver said under his breath.

Two cops came out carrying a woman on a stretcher. Then another couple of cops came out carrying a stretcher with a woman on it too. The stretchers were loaded into the back of the ambulance. The ambulance attendant climbed in and the doors slammed shut and the cops held their palms out to the driver to send them off.

Jerry backed away and the ambulance joined the traffic on Broadway.

'I'm sorry to tell ya,' one cop said to the other one. 'I've seen this before. It's too late for them.'

Jerry's eyes clouded over. He grabbed my arm and guided me toward Broadway, but there were no taxis. There were never yellow taxis uptown. We were going to have to find a gypsy cab, and you had to look hard for them, because they weren't real taxis – they were unlicensed, unmarked.

There was a man behind us hailing every single car that went by.

'Hey,' Jerry asked the man. 'You looking for a taxi?'

The man nodded. He had wild eyes, an edgy walk. He looked like he'd been punched in the stomach.

'You going to the hospital?' Jerry asked.

The man nodded.

'We're going there too.'

'There's a taxi!' I screamed, and hailed a big, old gray Impala. We all got in.

'I'm Jerry Hill,' said Jerry, turning to the man. 'And this here is Hannah.'

The man stared straight ahead, his face ashen.

'Landlord,' he mumbled.

'What?' Jerry asked.

'Landlord,' said the man, 'gave me a present.'

Jerry watched him and asked warily, 'What do you mean?'

'The landlord gave me a present.'

Jerry didn't say anything.

'I got a dead mother and sister. Landlord gave me a present,' the man said again.

I looked at Jerry, who covered his face with his hands. I looked out the window. Broadway was a blur, the blur a blessing because it wiped everything out.

'Landlord gave me a present. Landlord gave me a Christmas present.'

'I heard you,' Jerry said now. 'We're gonna be at the hospital soon.'

'I got a dead mother and sister,' said the man. 'Landlord gave me a present.'

Jerry told me to stay in the waiting room when we got to the hospital. He went into the ward with the man from the taxi. I sat in one of the plastic chairs. Stretchers glided past me. A man in a wheelchair screaming disappeared behind double doors. A doctor complained to a nurse that he couldn't stand seeing one more gunshot wound that night. Then I got up and wandered unnoticed in that way children can. I felt for the crucifix in my pocket. I stroked my fingers over its pewter curves for the last time before I put it into the garbage can.

Anyway, that's what happens when I try to write a Christmas story.

I know – you wanted something magical, and hopeful, and heartening. You wanted something for the kids. And I don't have anything against that. I don't even have anything against the gifts and the music and the tree. Sometimes I even go into the living room when I wake up in the middle of the night, and, while you're still sleeping, I plug in the Christmas lights and look at them blinking in the dark. And my heart goes, boom boom. I imagined a life like this when I was a kid.

But now – it's just not a good fit now. It's just not what I want.

I know that this place demands mandatory cheerfulness, and that this time of year there are so many people pretending excitement when they feel none. And I know how many people there are who are barely surviving, broke and hating everything about their lives, or trying to survive in a violent family. And I know the pressure to say everything's okay and everyone's at peace and everything's holy this time of year is bullshit – everything is not.

You will not be able to leave here, or at least you won't be able to leave here for a long time – not if you want be a father to Emma and Rosa (and you do).

I will not be able to stay here. It's not that I want to go back to where I grew up. I don't want to go back to that time and place ever again. I just don't want to be somewhere that erases that time and place. I don't want to be somewhere that erases stories like this one.

DANGERS OF THE SUN

When I tell you I'm taking time off to go to Vermont, where my childhood friend lives, you're probably picturing an old farmhouse in a snowy field, a Volvo out front and a rustic barn. But Reeny and the kids live in one of the two-story houses in Furnace Street, built when the paper mill was still going strong. The mill is gone now. The supermarket is closed too. Every house on the street is broken and damaged in its own way. I recognize the pattern of shingles patching Reeny's roof, the patch job that her husband did before he died. The window frames were repaired with unpainted wood. *It's a fixer upper that's never been fixed up*, Reeny would quip. The inside of the house is a maze of laundry baskets, dirty dishes, and empty pizza boxes. The kids' toys inhabit forgotten corners.

I'm on my way to Reeny's from New York, on the Ethan Allen Express, a train I haven't been on in years. It's the same train that Reeny and I used to take when we were kids going up to see her cousins, getting away from the city, leaving our parents behind.

When I tell you that Reeny and I used to visit Vermont when we were growing up in New York, you're probably picturing us with ruddy faces and crew neck sweaters. But we were from Washington Heights. When we went to Vermont, we wore tight jeans and slogan t-shirts, military surplus boots and backpacks. Two fourteen-year-old girls on their own – leaving the city. We were on guard the whole time. We wanted every other passenger on the train to know we would not abide their bullshit – especially the businessmen who got off at Croton-on-Hudson.

A lifetime has gone by since then. We both left New York – Reeny for Vermont, and me for Massachusetts. I went to college there, working two jobs at a time to supplement my scholarship. Then I went to grad school in Italy, worked for a museum in London, and came back to Massachusetts again before returning to New York. You might think I've come full circle; I haven't. The New York I live in is nothing like the New York that Reeny and I grew up in. I'm a curator at the Gowanus Museum and Art Gallery and I share a brownstone with four happy people who grew up in the suburbs.

There's a man in my life named Ray but we have not defined our relationship. In fact, I'm not sure what to call him, so I call him Ray. Acquaintances sometimes observe I am living like a student, as if I am afflicted with a condition of some sort that has held me back from advancing my own narrative. The more intrusive ones ask me what I'm waiting for. You might be wondering this too.

And Reeny?

Reeny has three children. Her husband died last year. I'm traveling to Vermont to attend his wrongful death trial.

Reeny and the children are waiting at the train station when I arrive. Since Richard died, Reeny's lost the plumpness she gained after the children were born. Her jeans hang on her. Her eyes are shadowed in purple and narrowed somehow. Her hair falls just past her shoulders, smooth and chestnut brown. Automatically, I reach out to hug her, then remember that I should move quickly because she doesn't like hugs. She reaches for a packet of rolling tobacco in the pocket of her leather jacket. She's begun smoking again.

When I tell you about how Richard died, you'll ask me to repeat what I've just told you. You'll want me to explain what malignant melanoma is. You'll tell me you didn't know that skin cancer can kill you. I'll tell you most don't, but malignant melanoma can, especially if it's not dealt with right away. Why didn't they deal with it? you'll ask. And I'll tell you about the doctor who thought Richard's mole was nothing to worry about, who only diagnosed it two years later, after the mole had grown. 'It was stage four by then,' I'll say. And there is no stage five and blahdy blahdy blah. You will look so far away, probably thinking about the imperfections on your own skin, until you return and ask, how old are the children?' 'They're eleven, nine, and five now,' I'll tell you

You will tell me it's a tragedy.

You will tell me you are so sorry. It will be busy, loud, lower Manhattan on a weekday after work. And you won't realize how, after that, there is nothing left for me to say.

You'll talk about your trip to Thailand, and I'll be thinking about biopsies. You'll talk about the personal ad you just took out, and I'll be thinking about chemo. You'll talk about the job you want to quit, and I'll be thinking about Reeny and the kids. You'll see my face stiffen, my eyes widen, and you won't understand my anger.

You'll ask me, 'Mia, what's wrong?'

Lena's the first one I see – the youngest, in a puffy pink coat, with messed up sandy hair. 'You're late,' she sings sweetly.

'The train was late,' Reeny corrects. She turns to me. 'You didn't try to slow the engineer down? Did you?'

'I didn't,' I confirm.

There's a sprinkling of snow on the ground, barely there. We walk toward Reeny's old Subaru. A whistle blows and the train pulls away. Its light slinks up the length of track, recedes from us.

'You staying for the whole trial?' Eric asks. He's tall for his age, lopes the way his father did. His father's black knit hat covers his smooth brown hair.

'It depends how long the trial is,' I answer.

'It's not going to be the trial of the century,' Reeny assures him.

'What was the trial of the century?' Grace asks – the middle child, big for her age, sullen. She speaks with a heavy Vermont accent that neither of the other children, or her parents, have. Reeny doesn't know where she picked it up.

'O. J. Simpson,' I say.

'Scopes Monkey Trial!' corrects Reeny.

'Oh shit!' I laugh.

We get into the car, explain the Scopes Monkey Trial, telling the kids about the teacher who was prosecuted for teaching evolution. We tell them that in Tennessee in 1925 some people got angry about the idea that human beings evolved from ape-like ancestors. Human beings descended from Adam and Eve, they said.

'That's stupid,' Grace comments from the back, as we drive along the main street. The town is dark and silent, the houses dim and unwelcoming. Their windows masked behind plastic sheets to keep out the cold.

There was a brilliant lawyer named Clarence Darrow who defended the teacher, Reeny continues, but the teacher was still found guilty. He didn't have to go to prison though, I add. The judge fined the teacher only $100.

Reeny and I knew about the Scopes Monkey Trial from watching *Inherit the Wind* again and again on TV in her parents' living room, the old black-and-white set broadcasting blue into the darkness at night, our introduction to justice sandwiched between ads for Alka Seltzer and Bounty Paper Towels.

When we arrive at the house, the kids pull off their

rubber boots. They shrug out of their down coats and throw them into the armchair that Richard used to sit in.

'Close the door behind you,' Reeny reminds them.

Eric turns on the TV and Reeny hands out pudding cups.

'Beer?' Reeny asks me. She opened a Molson for us each and we drink them out of the bottles.

Lena pirouettes over the scattered toys in her pink skirt. 'I'm a dancer,' she explains to me.

After the kids finish their pudding cups, Reeny tells them it's time for bed.

'But Mia's visiting,' Grace argues. 'We haven't seen her in a long time.'

'*I* haven't seen her in a long time,' Reeny snaps back. '*You* have to go to bed.'

Grace slumps her shoulders, sticks out her lower lip.

'Mom,' Eric asks. 'Can I come with you tomorrow?'

Reeny's eyes darken as she looks at him and a flicker of fear crosses his face. 'You have school tomorrow,' she snaps.

'But I want to come to court,' Eric insists.

'Upstairs,' Reeny orders. 'All of you. Now.'

Eric walks dejectedly to his room, climbs the steps slowly, his head down.

When I tell you that it was not Reeny's idea that I come for the trial, but her lawyer's idea instead, you might wonder what our friendship is like. We grew up blocks from each other, practically in one another's houses. That is, I grew up in her house. My family lived east of Broadway, and hers lived west, which was different territory. Her family was the lucky family. Hardworking happy dad who you hardly ever saw, but when you did, he was all: *Hi kids!* And: *You're going out? Good, have fun!*

'Is Mia staying for dinner?' Betty, Reeny's mom, used to ask. I was. Almost every single night. And Betty always came through. She cooked cheap, but there was always food on the table: salad with iceberg lettuce that she got from the vegetable man's bargain bin, lasagna made with Sloan's brand cottage cheese and, my favorite (which Betty knew) – frozen cheese ravioli with tomato sauce. She always managed to come up with something vegetarian for me, and this in a time and place where vegetarians were an oddity.

She was smiley, cheerful.

'What's she always so happy about?' my father complained once.

It was true that Betty's happiness hid some worry. The neighborhood concerned her – the petty and not-so-petty crime, the hold-ups and the drug distribution. She told Reeny and me not to go to the park. Of course we went to the park. We smoked pot there. She told us not to talk to the boys from Haven Avenue. Of course those were the boys we smoked pot with. Betty volunteered with the Girl Scouts. She helped with Girl Scout cookie sales. Sometimes there was a tall stack of Girl Scout cookies in Reeny's bedroom. Reeny and I would come home with terrible cases of the munchies, unable to think of anything but the chocolate covered Thin Mints. But all we could do was try not to look at them and wait for dinner.

Betty was also the Avon Lady – she went door to door to sell their stuff. We used the Skin So Soft as mosquito repellent. Betty was raising money for Catholic school tuition. She didn't want Reeny or her sister to go to George Washington High School. She'd seen the problems the boys had there and knew it would be worse for girls, so she decided she was going to send Reeny to Mother Cabrini. Reeny understood the need for this, but found it hilarious anyway. Her mother went to church because her mother's friends went to church, but no one in the house was religious. The week before Reeny started, an aunt came by and gave Reeny a book about the lives of the saints. Reeny and I read it out loud to one another while we were high, astounded by the terrible things that happened to the saints. 'Saint Perpetua and her slave Felicity were thrown naked into an arena with a wild cow,' Reeny read laughing, tears streaming down her face. 'Saint Eulalia was rolled down the street in a barrel full of knives.'

We couldn't breathe we were laughing so hard.

I said, 'Uh oh. You're gonna have to be careful in that school.'

I was going to start school at West Side Creative, which was one of the 'selective' schools – you passed a test and gave them a portfolio of your work. They took kids from all over the city and it was considered a prestigious place to go. They didn't charge tuition. Talent from everywhere, they said. 'How the hell did you get in there?' my father wanted to know. Betty thought it was great. Reeny's father told me to *have fun there*.

Reeny and I still hung out, even after we started going to different schools. It was mostly on weekends. And for the first time, I started spending time with Reeny's cousins too. Reeny really got to know them when they were all at Mother Cabrini. They lived further uptown, and they used to just show up every now and then. But for a while, all of us got together on weekends, going to Fordham Road in the Bronx. We used to go see movies and get ice cream there. And the cousins used to talk about the other cousins, the ones on the Island. And that's when I realized Betty Dennehy, who I always thought was Irish American like Reeny's dad, was from Puerto Rico. And when the cousins laughed about Tia Betty failing to wake up in time for a dawn festival in Ponce she starred in as a girl, they were talking about Reeny's mom. Betty never talked about Puerto Rico with us, ever. And I was even older before I understood why Betty used to tell Reeny and me to make to make sure we weren't out in the sun too long. 'This one,' she'd say, reaching for Reeny affectionately. 'She'll get too dark.'

Reeny and I lost touch for a while in our twenties, then found each other again a few years later. Eric was almost three by then, and Grace was going to be born soon. I was back in the US and living in Breeston, Massachusetts, which of course had the university. And everyone told me I was lucky to get a job at the Breeston Gallery of Contemporary Art. In fact, they told me I was lucky to live there at all. We were all lucky to live there. But I didn't feel lucky. I felt bored. And I felt like I didn't belong there. I felt like I couldn't tell the truth about where I was from. Everyone else there had stories about suburban childhoods. And everyone else kept talking about how good it was to be in a place that was as beautiful as Breeston, with such good people around. And I couldn't take it anymore. And one morning I woke up and decided it was time to move back to New York.

'Why?' Reeny asked.

I talked about returning to a place I'd run away from, wanting to see what the city was like as a grownup, wanting to revisit the places Reeny and I used to go, wanting to settle scores with a city that almost defeated me once. But the truth was less complicated than that. I missed the city where I'd grown up. It belonged to me, and I belonged to it, more than I'd realized before.

I was at the museum when Reeny phoned. She never usually phoned me at work. When I asked her if she was okay, she started to giggle. And then, with uncharacteristic sheepishness, she told me she had a favor to ask. Would it be possible for me to attend the trial that was coming up?

'Of course,' I said. I'd already offered to but she'd said she didn't need anyone there. It was just, she explained, that her lawyer thought she should have someone in the courtroom with her.

Of course she should have someone there with her, I confirmed.

No, she said. What she meant was, she didn't feel like she had to have someone there with her, but her lawyer wanted her to because, if she didn't, the jury might think she didn't have any friends. And that, her lawyer said, would make them think something was wrong.

I told her I wanted to be there.

She didn't know anyone else who could attend every day, because her friends there couldn't get time off from work.

I told her I was sure the museum would understand. I could probably even do some of the planning for the next exhibition from there. I'd bring the museum's laptop along.

The whole thing was stupid, she said – it was just a trial. Why should people have to take time off from work?

It was fine, I said. It was no problem at all. I wanted to be there.

The clerk tells us to rise and we rise in the nearly empty courtroom. I'm in the second row of benches, behind Reeny, who sits at the plaintiff's table, shoulders hunched in her maroon cardigan. Her lawyer, Ben, is next to her. He rises to give his opening statement.'Ladies and gentlemen, this doctor still has not taken responsibility for what he's done, still has not tried to make amends for his misjudgment.' He's stocky and dark-haired and looks like a boy in his charcoal-colored suit.

The doctor sits at the defendant's table with a dazed smile, hands folded like an attentive schoolboy. Reeny notes he is dressed in Brooks Brothers – the shirt, the jacket, pants

– all of it. She spent a summer working at a country club in Connecticut, got good at classifying who was who and who wore what, who belonged and who got snubbed. Was he from a good family? Did he underperform in medical school? Is he in central Vermont because he likes it, or because he couldn't get a job anywhere else. He seems inscrutable sitting there, blinking his bland blue eyes. How could he have changed the course of Richard's life, or Reeny's life?

The doctor's attorney is corpulent, in a suit with a 1980s cut that's slightly too small; nearly finished with middle-age. I imagine him going to the steakhouse where he's a regular. He orders a scotch, a Diet Coke on the side. He goes through his papers, drinks the Coke, drinks the scotch. The waitress knows his order before he gives it. He's there every day after work. He tells his wife he's working late, but he's really reading the paper there, biding his time. Sometimes one of the other regulars stops by to say hello. When he gets home, his wife will be watching TV, rapt as she sits on the living room couch. She will not turn her head when he walks in. It is better this way for both of them.

And the judge? She reminds me of the kind of people I worked for when I was a student, when I used to cut hedges, pull weeds, spread landscape bark. Someone like her used to come out of the kitchen, look around, narrow her eyes, ask if I was thirsty and wanted something to drink. Out of spite I would say no. I would see them over and over – those slim, patrician women with shoulder-length gray hair. They would compliment me about something mundane, and if I didn't respond, compliment me again. She reminds me of the kind of person who thinks her opinion is worth more than others people's opinions. Then I remind myself that, in this case, it is.

During the first bathroom break, Reeny offers this observation about the jury: 'They're all wearing their Christmas best.' And she's right. Their flannel shirts with just-unpackaged folds. Their chinos are wrinkle free. They're wearing the kind of sweaters that are too uncomfortable to wear on a regular basis. Were they ordered around by idiotic bosses at UPS, talked down to by bank managers when they wanted loans for their farms, screamed at by someone wanting a special order at D'Angelo's? The judge and two lawyers are focusing all their attention on the jurors, pleading with them, reasoning with them, and advising them that this decision – determining who was responsible for Richard Kozak's death – is theirs. And the jurors, in turn, look embarrassed to be at the center of attention like this, surprised by the respect being shown to them, daunted by the role they must play.

I'd first learned about the diagnosis on the same day Reeny and Richard had. I had just come home from work, the long commute. The walk back to my apartment had been peaceful and calming. The neighbors sat on their stoops and nodded and smiled as I walked past. Some little girls were playing nearby and laughing while they ran up the sidewalk. I climbed the steps to the brownstone. No one else was home yet. My bedroom overlooked the backyard, and I was on the top floor, so it was quiet there. The sky was so smogged, it looked as if someone had taken a steel wool pad and rubbed it until it had gone gray. It was familiar and comforting to me, and I was glad I had moved back to New York.

The phone rang, and Reeny's voice tripped out quickly, and she began by informing me: 'The doctor told him it was nothing to worry about.'

She was the one who'd noticed the mark on Richard's back. Richard sat up in bed, and she saw the strange mole, and it looked like the one she'd seen in the magazine article on skin cancer – like the image in the magazine she'd picked up at work. She wanted him to get it checked.

When she got home that night, she asked him if he'd phoned the clinic. He had, he said, but there were no appointments. The doctor he normally went to was booked solid for months. 'Why don't you just go to the doctor who has appointments?' she asked.

'I don't know,' Richard said. 'I just don't like him.'

Did they have this conversation when he was standing in the kitchen, cracking his first beer of the night? Had the kids all rushed to him when he walked in the door, grabbing onto his dusty blue jeans? He was working at a ski resort that summer, replacing the asphalt shingles on the main lodge. There were guesthouses and buildings they called the villas and he had to drive seventy-five miles there and seventy-five miles back. He and his friend Bill started out at seven in the morning. He wanted to sit in his chair, turn on the TV, find an end to his day.

Reeny kept bothering him about seeing the doctor.

He made the appointment finally. It was with Dr. Dealy, the physician he felt funny about.

'The doctor said it was nothing to worry about,' Reeny repeated. And two years after he said that? Reeny could see that the thing had gotten bigger. They had better health insurance now. Maybe he could get the mole removed now so they wouldn't have to worry about it anymore.

Richard went back to Dr. Dealy – he still couldn't get an appointment with the doctor he liked. Dr. Dealy ordered a biopsy, and the results came back. It was malignant melanoma, stage four.

Reeny puts her hand on a Bible, says she swears to tell the truth. The doctor's attorney has called her to the stand. He asks her what the mole looked like. Her lower lip quivers and she freezes. She has always hated this – having everyone's eyes on her. One on one, she's self-assured as a cinematic private eye, the kind we used to worship when we were kids. Here, she keeps tugging at her sweater sleeves, leaning forward, looking down.

Ben has told her she should smile at the jury, and, periodically, out of context, she looks at them and gives them a tight, strained smile. Then she glances at Ben for approval. The doctor's attorney stands in front of her, waiting.

'It was three centimeters,' Reeny says softly.

'Mrs. Kozak,' the doctor's attorney asks, 'have you always used the metric system?'

Reeny, surprised by the question, answers, 'No.'

'You don't use the metric system.'

She answers, 'No.' Ben has told her to keep her answers as short as possible, to not explain anything that hasn't been asked.

'But you knew that *this* mole was three centimeters.'

'Yeah,' Reeny says.

The judge turns to her. 'Mrs. Kozak, for the purposes of the court report, I need you to say, yes instead of yeah.'

Reeny says, 'Yes.'

'But you didn't measure it,' the doctor's attorney asks, 'did you?'

'No,' Reeny says.

'Did somebody tell you it was three centimeters?' he asks.

'Your Honor,' Ben says, rising, 'Dr. Dealy's own record notes the mole was nearly three centimeters in size.'

'I'm trying to ascertain what the witness knew,' says the doctor's attorney. 'Not find out what Dr. Dealy's records stated at the time. Mrs. Kozak wouldn't have seen the records then.'

'Your Honor,' Ben says, standing, 'Mr. Stanley is attempting to impeach Mrs. Kozak. I have to object to this line of questioning.'

Ben was Richard's high school buddy. Did he envy Richard's bad boy status, his late-night rides and paper-bag-sheathed bottles, his stoned who-gives-a-fuck attitude in math class? Richard, so big and tall; the school basketball star. Ben must have known enough to envy Richard's standing at school. But not his home life, anything but his home life: his bad luck mother with her string of mean boyfriends, their backhanded greetings when Richard walked in at night.

And Ben – Ben was the kind of guy whose parents were always proud of him – even before he took the LSATs on a dare. They wanted him to take over the farm, but they understood when he went to law school instead. Ben, and his high school sweetheart wife, his two toddlers, his third baby on the way.

One day Richard came into the office explaining he needed more than a DWI defense this time. And Ben said, yes, he could help Richard out. He left the law firm he'd worked for since law school. He went forty-five thousand dollars into debt for research and expert witnesses. He was going to fight for Richard and Reeny. I think of him as that kind of lawyer: the kind who believes that with enough passion and smarts, you can put things right. Because every client who walked into his office in dust-covered jeans, mud-caked boots, a cow-smelling jacket was him, him – if he hadn't taken up that dare, if he had not gotten that score and the LSATs and left the county for three years so he could get his law degree.

Ben is playing a video of Richard for the courtroom. It was shot two months before Richard died so that Ben and the doctor's attorney could ask Richard questions they would not be able to ask him if he died before the case went to trial.

Richard appears on the screen with rings under his eyes, his head shaved, his big hands folded. Ben's voice come from off screen, gently asks Richard, 'Do you remember what Dr. Dealy told you when you showed him the mole?'

'He said it was nothing to worry about,' Richard tells him. His voice catches in anger.

'You're sure of that?' Ben asks.

'I remember it exactly,' Richard says. 'He said it was nothing to worry about.'

'Did he say anything else, Richard?'

'He said that I could get the mole removed if I wanted to. You know, if it was making me uncomfortable.'

'What did you say when he told you that, Richard?'

'I asked him if my insurance would cover it. He said he didn't know. But he said it was nothing to worry about.'

Reeny does not react, at all, while she is watching the video. She has seen it many times. She has played it on the VCR at home, after the kids have gone to sleep. She has left it on while she drifts off to sleep so she can hear Richard's voice again, as if he were in the room with her.

'If his family didn't have so much bad luck, they wouldn't have had any luck at all,' Reeny used to say, rolling her eyes. It was an old joke, but the only way to start the story. Richard's father had been injured in Korea, not so badly that he qualified for full disability, but badly enough so he always had trouble working after that. Richard's mother and her boyfriend were killed in a car accident, but Richard believed the boyfriend deliberately drove off a cliff to kill them both. Richard had grown up in a trailer park, on the outskirts of town. He and his brother and his sisters all went to an evangelical church when they were growing up because the kids who went there could get a free McDonald's meal. He'd been working as a roofer since high school, working with his uncle who told him he should do roofing when he was young. You didn't want to do it when you got old, didn't want to risk falling off a roof. It wasn't fun, but it was steady work.

And then he got the prognosis: stage four melanoma is very difficult to cure because it has already spread to other parts of the body. However, a small number of people respond well to treatment, achieve No Evidence of Disease and survive for many years following diagnosis. Researchers are also working every day to improve the durability of response and increase the number of people who benefit from treatment. The five-year overall survival ranges between 5 and 19%, depending on the location and number of metastases and associated systemic changes.

He contacted Ben. Ben got a response from the doctor's insurance company. They were willing to pay $300,000 in compensation. They had calculated that this would be equivalent to Richard's lifetime earnings as a roofer. After all, he couldn't have kept doing it as he got older. They said this amount would meet the needs of Mr. Kozak's wife and his three children.

When I tell you that the doctor's attorney calls Dr. Dealy 'Doc' during the trial, you might think I've got it wrong. You might think that sounds facile, hammy, amateurish. But that's what the doctor's attorney does. He asks: 'You doing okay, Doc?' And when the courtroom breaks for lunch. 'Make sure you get back early. Okay, Doc?' And he always says it loud enough for everyone to hear. When he wants Dr. Dealy to give testimony, he says, 'Time for you to take the witness stand, Doc.'

Reeny notes that the doctor has shaved his beard for the trial, has cut his hair, has bought new glasses. There is no sign of the Humvee he used to drive around town. Yes, a Humvee. He has a Ford Taurus now. He also has a fiancée. The woman in the red wool suit, who showed up with her hair in a twist on the first day, looking like she was ready for cocktails. Someone must have told her not to dress that way, Reeny guesses, because after that first day, she wears corduroy jumper dresses instead, LL Bean turtlenecks, carries a plaid wool shawl – the sort you see in catalogues for city people who want to live a country lifestyle.

The fiancée looks dewy-eyed as Dr. Dealy takes the witness stand. She pulls her shawl around her shoulders.

'Doc,' the doctor's attorney says. 'Do you remember asking Mr. Kozak if he had been sunburned when he was a child?'

'I didn't have to,' Dr. Dealy answers. He pauses. 'I knew he'd been sunburned – with his coloring. And I knew he didn't wear a shirt when he worked as a roofer.'

'That's a risk factor for melanoma, isn't it?'

'It is,' says Dr. Dealy.

'And do you remember what you told Mr. Kozak when he was ready to leave your office that day?'

'I told him to keep an eye on the mole, to watch it.'

'To look for changes?'

'Yes, I told him to look for changes. To see if it grew bigger, if it changed shape, if it grew darker.'

'But the mole was on Mr. Kozak's back,' notes the doctor's attorney. 'How could he have watched for changes?'

'Well, he couldn't have,' Dr. Dealy says, as if they were discussing this for the first time. 'Someone else would have to look for him.'

'Who were you expecting to look for changes?' the doctor's attorney asks.

'His wife,' says Dr. Dealy.

The doctor's attorney looks at his notes, then at Dr. Dealy again.

'And Mrs. Kozak did notice a change, didn't she?'

'Yes. Almost two years later.'

'So Mr. Kozak came back to your office.'

'Almost two years later.'

'And did the mole look to you as if it had changed?'

'Oh my,' says Dr. Dealy. 'Yes. It was twice as large as it had been. Three centimeters now, and it had blood coming from it.'

'And what was your reaction?' the doctor's attorney asks.

'I knew it wasn't good,' says Dr Dealy, who looks solemnly at his attorney, 'I knew it wasn't good. I felt terrible that Mr. Kozak hadn't come in sooner.'

His attorney nods at him, as if he has said exactly what he was supposed to say.

His attorney nods at him, as if he has said exactly what he was supposed to say.

When I tell you about the time that Reeny and I got jumped when we were kids, you might wonder, why this and why now? And I'll tell you, 'Because we grew up evaluating risk. We did not think we were safe from anything, ever, and I need to you understand this.'

And you'll say, 'What do you mean you were jumped?'

And I'll say, 'What do you think I mean?'

And you'll say, 'You mean like, assaulted?'

And I'll say, 'Yeah, like assaulted.'

Did they touch your private parts? the kind and reassuring cops asked us.

We were delivering Avon for Betty, going over to some of the apartment buildings east of Broadway, even further east than where I lived. It was a bad street in a bad neighborhood. But Betty had an emergency and couldn't make it, and Reeny knew the route. She'd gone with Betty sometimes. And suddenly, there are all these boys. There were these boys surrounding us in the building shouting, *Oh boy, the Avon Ladies!*

When I tell you about this, you're gonna think this is the part where we got, you know, assaulted. But it was just the first time, because that's what happened everywhere, all the time. That's what happened over and over again.

We'd go to meet Reeny's cousins, and some guy on the street would stand in the way and ask, *Are you girls looking for something?*

We'd walk down Broadway on a hot summer's day and we'd hear the kissing sounds and the mamis and the miras and try not to look.

We'd go into the bodega and the guy behind the counter would aim receipt paper at Reeny's chest.

Even when we went downtown, there were sleazes in business suits. One day we were walking through Penn Station when a Connecticut commuter brushed past us breathing *nice* into our faces. He had his hand jammed into his open fly, like a pervert version of Napoleon Bonaparte, a suburban fuck feeling himself up. Reeny and I ran away laughing with fear. Then, about ten minutes later, we saw him again on the concourse, holding his briefcase with that filthy hand, looking up at the departures board. I had a little leather bag on a long strap, and when my keys and my change were in it, it was heavy – a weapon. So I whapped him. His hand went up to his neck and he looked around but he didn't see us. And Reeny and I ran away, laughing. He literally didn't know what hit him.

We spent a lot of time back at Reeny's watching Humphrey Bogart movies. All sorts of shit happened to Bogart, but he just kept on going. He never stopped, never cried, always had a good comeback. He'd say: 'Such a lot of guns around town and so few brains!' And he'd say: 'I don't mind a reasonable amount of trouble.' And he'd say: 'Things are never so bad they can't be made worse.' Betty was glad we were safe there at home, watching TV in the living room. She even let us have some of the Girl Scout cookies. And she never ever again asked us to deliver Avon.

'How would you girls like to go up to Vermont?' Reeny's father asked us one day. 'You know you've got cousins there.'

The Vermont Dennehies thought we were hilarious. They thought we were kidding when we said we'd never seen a cow in real life. They thought our worries about taking a shortcut through the woods at night were a joke. They thought we were teasing them when we asked if a swimming hole was the same thing as a lake. But when we lifted our faces to the sky that first night and we gasped at the number of stars in the sky – stars shining in a darkness it was impossible to find in a city – they realized we weren't joking.

We did not know any of the things they were showing us. We were amazed by all of it.

The cousins really ran a general store, and that really was where people in town bought everything, and we could really go behind the counter and serve ice cream to customers.

And of course we could come back there, Reeny's old cousin said. Their great-grandfather had bought this place because he wanted his family to have some land after he had to leave Ireland, and he would want everyone to come there.

Whenever I am on a train snaking across the countryside – in Italy, or England, or back in America again – I remember that first train ride, the one Reeny and I took to Vermont and how, when we looked out that window and saw the buildings became smaller smaller, when we could feel the chill of the window as we put our foreheads against it, we understood we were going somewhere safer than we'd ever been before.

Reeny's friends come to court – usually just for a few hours at a time, during an afternoon off work, a morning away from the kids. Some are witnesses.

'What did Richard say after the doctor's visit?' Ben asks them.

The judge and attorneys have long conferences over whether this is hearsay while Joe, Richard's best friend, is stuck sitting in the witness stand.

'Did Reeny and Richard's marriage appear to be a happy one?' the doctor's attorney asks.

Ben objects, calling the questioning irrelevant.

'Your Honor, the plaintiff opened this line of questioning when he asked witnesses to testify about the relationship between Mr. Kozak and Mrs. Kozak.'

The judge, her face frozen in thought, agrees.

Reeny goes running off to the conference room during the break, fists clenched.

We – Ben, Joe, and I – follow her into that airless room with its big table and portraits of past judges,. We slip in as fast as possible and shut the door.

'So what?' Reeny wants to know. 'If we fought, does that mean I killed him?'

Ben puts his hand on Reeny's back. Reeny stiffens. 'It just makes them look bad,' he assures her.

She's looking into Joe's eyes, Joe, who with his jaw clenched, had wept on the stand.

'You did good in there,' Ben assures him.

He gives Ben a half smile.

Before court began, Ben was begging Joe to cut his ponytail off. He'd argued with Reeny about it, who informed him she wasn't going to tell her friends to cut their hair and buy new clothes to testify. The jury dressed in jeans, Reeny pointed out. But that was the jury, Ben responded.

I could see Ben's shoulders tighten sometimes when Reeny's friends came in. He'd asked Reeny teasingly once, at the end of one of their arguments, 'Is Sherry's hair still purple?'

The work wardrobe that I'd brought with me – the jackets and skirts I hated – was silently approved of by Ben, an example of what he wanted to see more of: middle-class respectability, Exhibit A.

'You did good,' he says to Joe again.

Joe is weeping, reaching up to wipe the tears from his eyes.

And I realize, watching him, watching Reeny's other friends, how little I was present for, how much they have witnessed, how much they have seen as Richard's life slipped away.

The beating summer rain – a flash flood. They were in the Subaru, the better car, the one with brakes, driving home from the hospital. They had told him, you have – maybe – six months to live. We thought you would have longer. We told you you'd have longer, but it's gone to your brain now. This is the result of the MRI. They have told him this, him and Reeny, and they sat in the solid wood chairs before the doctor's desk, nodding, asking questions whose answers were never the right ones. And, in the parking lot, the sky darkened. Too late for omens, Reeny thought. Even that was fucking late. They were late to pick up the children, visiting Denise and her kids in the trailer down the street. And the sky had been so brilliant blue it hurt to look at it when they left, so cotton candy clean it barely seemed real. But now there's the rain, and the Subaru doesn't like rain, should have its catalytic converter replaced, can stall in heavy, humid air. And it does. Just as they're turning onto the highway, the car stalls and it won't start up again. And she sees the look on Richard's face, not believing that this can happen too. And she looks out again at the rain, torrential, the speeding cars slapping air and streams of mud at their car. And she says to him, 'I guess this is what you'd call having a bad day.'

And he bursts into tears then, starts to weep.

If only she wasn't trying to be Humphrey fucking Bogart, he wouldn't have to do all the weeping.

'Please rise for the judge.'

We rise, sit, rise, just like good little schoolchildren.

I've been trying to work at night, with the laptop balanced on my knees, while Reeny and the kids watch TV, but it's hard to. Somewhere along the way, I've lost a folder with printouts of the text for the exhibition. I keep trying to imagine where it could be, and my mind is racing. My skirt hangs, looking for lost weight. Something's irritating my eyes and I rub them more than I should. My jacket needs dry cleaning.

I search the faces of the jury – try to keep track of when they look interested, when they look sad. Ben quizzes me on this regularly. There's the old man whose face droops with disappointment. Every now and then he looks my way. There's the woman with home-permed hair who looks as if she won't let you get away with anything, so don't you even try it. There's the young guy whose skin gets ruddy without instigation. Ben has nicknamed them all – Mr. Droop, Aunt Nasty, Rusty. He's not interested in appearing compassionate anymore. He just wants justice, and all the barriers to it are making him angry. 'We'll get that bastard,' he assures Reeny. He paces while he plans. His suit is growing too large. His hair is uncombed and bristly.

And I think, Hey, Mr. Married Attorney Who Is Representing my Childhood Friend – I'm starting to find you really sexy.

When I tell you that the doctor's attorney also plays a video of Richard, you might at first – as I did – wonder what he's doing. Isn't the testimony of a dead man going to damn the defendant? But a different section of Richard's deposition has been queued up. There's Richard again, looking exhausted, hollow-eyed. But the doctor's attorney is the one whose voice you can hear from off-screen.

'Mr. Kozak, what was your reaction when the doctor told you your prognosis?'

Richard looks up, the colors slightly off on the monitor this time – the reds just pink, the neutral tones slightly green.

'When he told me I was going to die?' Richard asks, squinting slightly as if looking into light.

'Yes.'

'I… I was thinking about Reeny and the kids. I was worried about how Reeny was going to be. I didn't know how she was going to manage.'

'What did you do when you got home, Mr. Kozak?'

'When I got home?'

'Did you talk to your wife?'

'Of course.'

'And did you make repairs on the house?'

Richard looks bewildered for a minute. How does the doctor's attorney know this?

Richard says, 'Yeah. I went up to the roof and put some new shingles on. I fixed one of the windows.'

'Because you didn't think Mrs. Kozak would be able to manage on her own.'

Richard starts to weep.

'I felt like I let them down.' He covers his face with his hands. 'I let them down,' he sobs.

The doctor's attorney clicks on the remote, stops the tape.

I remember what she told me about Richard's last night:

She'd been sitting by his bed, holding his hand for hours. The painkillers made his speech soft and slippery. 'I'm scared,' he told her. Then, 'It was my bike.'

'I'm right here,' she reassured him, stroking his forehead, his bloated face.

Hallway light seeped into the room's dimness. A monitor beeped. Footsteps receded.

His breath came in with difficulty, left as if it was running away.

Snow was falling outside in the late late night, light and inconsequential. It made the sky impossible to characterize – it was neither clear nor stormy. There was neither a mouthful of bright stars nor a torrent of sharp sudden flakes. You couldn't see what phase the moon was in. The lamps illuminating the hospital's parking lot kept the darkness from ever being sure. Every now and then, a car pulled away, left the nearly empty lot and traveled toward the highway. They left no trails. The snow was blotted by the rough asphalt of the ground. It wouldn't stick. Reeny heard Richard's voice again and looked away from the window, looked at him, and remembered when, at nineteen, she'd wait for him at the Snail's Pace, hoping he'd be in that night, hoping he'd woo her with his snide, contrived cynicism and take her home. It wasn't love but comfort that brought her to him then. 'Richard,' she said stroking his forehead with her fingertips.

He'd closed his eyes. 'It's over,' he told her.

He breathed a few more times. And then he stopped.

Reeny squeezed his hand. He did not squeeze back.

The monitor let out its smooth, persistent whine. It was almost comforting in that moment.

Richard, completely still, completely silent, his hand still warm.

Then someone else appeared – a nurse. She walked over to Richard, checked his breathing, his pulse.

Reeny backed up to the window by then, eyes widened, and the nurse confirmed, 'He's gone.'

Reeny unclenched her hands, stepped forward from the windowsill. She looked at Richard again, his shaved head, tilted against the pillow in her direction.

'I'm sorry,' the nurse told Reeny. Dressed in white, just like a TV nurse. 'Do you want some time alone?' the nurse asked.

Reeny nodded, yes.

'Why don't I call someone to pick you up?' the nurse asked.

Reeny looked at her watch, a plastic digital with Power Rangers figures on it she took from Eric when she couldn't find her own. 'It's three AM,' she informed the nurse.

'I don't want you driving home alone,' the nurse told her. Gray curly hair, big brown eyes, and small but sturdy.

The nurse reminded Reeny of her mother. She opened her mouth to speak, stopped.

'Who do you want me to call?' the nurse asked again.

'Call the Black Horse,' Reeny said after a minute.

'The bar?' asked the nurse.

A bar open until four AM, just over the New York State border.

'My friend Sherry works there,' Reeny explained.

🔽

Ben knows that Reeny will freeze on the witness stand, does not want to explain the last weeks of Richard's life. But still, he has to put her on the stand.

'Did you bring the children to the hospital?' Ben asks her.

Reeny nods. 'We wanted them to be able to say goodbye.'

Reeny's tugging at her sleeves. Ben is trying to make her cry, but Reeny won't do it, not in front of all these people.

'What did Richard say to the children?'

Reeny shrugs. 'He said goodbye,' she whispers.

'How old are the children again?' Ben asks.

'Eleven, eight, and five. They were nine, six, and three at the time,' Reeny tells him. 'Lena – she's the youngest – wanted to get into the hospital bed with him.'

'And did she?' Ben asks.

Reeny nods.

'You have to say yes or no,' the judge reminds her.

'I'm sorry,' Reeny says. 'Yes.'

'Who brought the children?' Ben asks her.

'Our friends – Denise and her husband Joe.'

'And then they brought the children home?'

'Yes,' Reeny says.

'At midnight.'

'Yes.'

'And when did Richard die. What time was it?'

'Almost three AM,' says Reeny.

'Were you with him when he died?'

'Yes,' says Reeny.

'And did he say anything to you before he died?' Ben asks.

'He said, "It's over."'

'I have no further questions, Your Honor.'

Reeny and I go to Denise's to pick up the kids. The air is moist in there, a reprieve from the sharp chill outside. Denise sits on an afghan-covered sofa, grandmother-stained sateen concave in the middle. The children, Reeny's and Denise's, run back and forth in front of the television. Reeny delivers a report of the day's proceedings to Denise, who tells her youngest to leave Lena alone. Grace wriggles along the arm of a chair, watching *Mr. Ed* with grim fascination. 'Mommy, that horse doesn't look like it's talking really.'

Grace puts the top of her head in the seat of the chair, an aborted attempt at a handstand.

'Did you find your shoes?' Reeny asks. 'We have to go home.'

Grace stands. 'Mia,' she says. 'You haven't seen the kittens, have you?'

'There are kittens?' I ask.

Denise stubs out her cigarette. 'Joe found them out by the mill. Five of them and their mother.'

'Can I see them?'

'I'll take you,' Grace says eagerly.

'They're in the bathroom,' Denise says, with dread.

Grace starts sliding along the long hallway in her socks. I follow, hear Denise call out, 'It's messy.' Then, as

I am about to tell her it's nothing, she says to Reeny, 'I'm embarrassed to let Mia see it.'

And there's something terrible in me that's consoled by the fact that she thinks I'm someone she needs to clean up for. After feeling driven down all week, I feel stupidly high up. And Reeny must have picked up on that, must have regained the near telepathy we had when we were kids, because she tells Denise, 'If you saw where Mia grew up, you wouldn't be embarrassed about anything. I've never seen any place that filthy.'

So that when I am walking down the hall, I feel my face grow warm, just as it used to when I was a child, when shame washed over me again and again, washed over me every time someone saw how we lived. And even the tiny kittens, mewling and struggling in the towel-lined box, sinking their tiny claws into my hand, can't take that shame away.

Eric wakes in the night, his sharp voice cutting through my tense sleep. Desperately, he cries, 'Daddy! Daddy!' It takes me a minute to realize where I am. I stalk through the dark in my t-shirt and panties. By the time I arrive at Eric's room, Reeny is there holding him, and his sobs are more from excitement than terror. 'Daddy was here,' he tells her. 'Daddy,' he says again, looking at Reeny while tears roll down his face. The girls have gathered around, Lena pointing her toes and looking down, Grace sullenly shaking her head.

'You just had a dream,' Reeny tells her son, rubbing his back.

'Daddy's dead,' Grace confirms.

'Well,' Lena says, her voice tiny and snippy at the same time. 'I saw him too.'

We sit in the Subaru, in the gravel parking lot next to the refurbished Victorian building where Ben has an office. The sky, colorless as steel, is dropping pathetically small snowflakes. Reeny pulls her coat around her, the big wool one she bought when she was pregnant. 'I want the trial to be over,' she says.

'It will be,' I say, uselessly.

Of course it will be. She needs it to be over now.

A split has developed on my pantyhose. I touch it with my fingertip, on my thigh, needing to be sure it's not an optical illusion. It ends just at my hemline. I will have to keep pulling my skirt down to make sure it doesn't show.

Reeny stares ahead grimly, eyes damp, lipsticked mouth slightly open, as if she's about to speak. Her hair is caught in the collar of her coat, drapes around her face like a hood.

I ask, 'What?'

She shakes her head. 'I don't know. It's just weird. This whole thing scares me sometimes.'

'Me too,' I say. I grope for something else to say. 'The worst that can ever happen is someone can die,' I say finally. 'And that part's already happened.'

'I know,' says Reeny. 'But…' She turns to me, tears in her eyes pooling. 'What about Richard?'

'What do you mean?' I ask.

'What if we lose? What about him?'

'Richard would want you to give them a fight. Whether you win or not.'

But even as I say these words, I know how empty and scripted they sound. Richard was angry. He would have wanted Reeny to fight. And he would have wanted her to win. He would not have wanted her on the stand, having to describe every private moment to a jury, a judge, a corpulent and arrogant attorney. And, most of all, that doctor.

Every time we walk into the courthouse, the bailiff searches bags and file boxes for weapons, then waves us through the metal detector. I could do what Reeny does, not bring a bag in, but I want my bag there. I don't want to give in to implicit prohibition. The bailiff, with his edge of awkward adolescence, his boniness and crewcut, opens every zippered compartment on my leather backpack, jokes with me about whether I've brought hand grenades this time, and I give him the obligatory smile.

'He's flirting with you,' Reeny observes disapprovingly, once we get through.

'He's just bored,' I say, struggling to sound flip.

But I hate the way he looks in every part of the bag, shoving his big hands in the pockets on the side, slowly undoing the zippers.

The doctor's attorney is a lounge pianist with a big audience on the last performance – he's played this tune so many times and he know's he's good at it.

'Ladies and gentlemen of the jury, what happened to Mr. Kozak is a tragedy. No one is arguing that is wasn't, but Dr. Dealy is not responsible for that tragedy. Dr. Dealy did everything that he could as Mr. Kozak's physician. The rest of it was up to Mr. Kozak.'

This man looks just like those businessmen who hit on us as fourteen-year-old girls. I want to whap him with the leather bag I had when I was a girl, thwack him on the back of his head, make him feel something.

When Ben stands before the jury to give his summary, he suddenly seems robbed of all authority, a boy masquerading as an attorney, a boy who had to stay up all night to get ready for today. I don't want to see this, and I can't help thinking this. 'And if Dr. Dealy didn't think the mole was cancerous, then why did he ask Richard Kozak to keep an eye on it?' Ben asks the jury, palms open, as if waiting for them to throw their verdict so he can catch it.

I swallow. He's repeating a question that I asked rhetorically, once, with him and Reeny in the pub. Repeated here, in the courtroom, it sounds lightweight.

'You can't have it both ways,' Ben adds.

When I tell you that we go into the plaintiff counsel's conference room to wait for a verdict, you might be picturing us sitting there and speaking seriously, you might think of us telling revelatory stories about the past. But we're goofy by then, giddy. We start mimicking every courtroom drama we've ever seen.

'I want the truth!' Ben shouts.

'You can't handle the truth!' Reeny shouts back.

Reeny and I start singing, 'Here comes da judge. Here comes da judge.'

Ben sings back, 'Order in the court, the monkey wants to speak.'

We sit in that room lined with photos of former judges – judges with 1920s slicked hair and round wire glasses, judges with jolly 1950s crewcuts and neat little bowties, judges with 1970s side parts and shaggy eyebrows.

'Hey,' Ben asks. 'Your hands wet? Man, my palms are so damp, I don't think I can pick anything up anymore.'

I'm wiping my hands on the knees of my pantyhose. Yes, my hands are wet. Yes, I am sweating.

By seven we're too hungry to sit any longer without food. I leave the courthouse and walk down the dark hill to the sandwich shop, inching my high heels down the rain-slicked sidewalks. The sandwich shop glows yellow in the cold, sputtering rain. This is where Rutland's yuppies come for cappuccino and whole-meal muffins. A spike-haired woman in a big sweater sits speaking to a bearded man in a clean flannel shirt. A woman with gray wavy hair down to her waist rearranges some magazines. They are all oblivious to melanoma and trial verdicts. I take the sandwiches and leave, and when I get back to the courthouse I have to pound on the door to be let back into the building.

For a long time after it is over, I fantasize about being able to freeze frame our lives. And I imagine reaching into the frame to adjust things.

Dr. Dealy stands behind Richard, hand stopped in midair, mouth slightly open. Richard is upright, rigid, about to shiver from the touch of Dr. Dealy's hands, but he hasn't yet. To do that, I must hit the start button, and I won't do that until after I have made adjustments.

Here is what I have arranged:

Dr. Dealy has just been to a conference on melanoma. He is acutely aware of its warning signs. He woke that morning to find his lover brushing hair from his eyes. 'You're fine the way you are,' she tells him. 'I don't know why you worry about people liking you.' He's come to work happy and at peace with himself, treasuring the familiarity of the clinic, the traffic of townspeople he sees every week at Shaw's. When his assistant hands him the next file, he meets her eyes and thanks her, then goes to meet Richard in the waiting room. 'You're Eric's father?' Dr. Dealy asks. 'Aren't you? He's a smart kid.'

In the examination room, Richard undresses. Dr. Dealy, on the other side of the curtain, carefully goes over Richard's chart. 'Are you ready?' he calls out.

'Yup,' Richard says.

Dr. Dealy slides open the curtain.

Richard is sitting on the examination table, tufted vinyl sticking to his skin where the gown begins to spread.

'Let's take a look at that mole,' says Dr. Dealy.

He stands behind Richard.

I hit the start button.

Dr. Dealy slides open the back of Richard's gown, touches the mole.

Richard shivers.

'Here?' Dr. Dealy asks.

'Yeah,' Richard says, before the stretch of wordlessness, the moment in which all background sound – the rustle of papers, his palm unpuckering from the vinyl, Dr. Dealy's footsteps – is amplified.

Dr. Dealy stands before him, saying, 'Let's get that biopsied. It might be not anything at all, but we want to make sure.And if there is a problem, we want to make sure we catch it early. I don't want you to go home worrying about this. Skin cancer isn't a problem if you catch it early.We don't know what this is yet, but let's make sure, okay?'

Dr. Dealy numbs Richard's lower back with Novocain, slides the blade against the mole, and slips it into a clear plastic container. In four days, the results of the biopsy will be returned – local melanoma, stage one.

He will be given the prognosis for stage one melanoma: with appropriate treatment, stage one melanoma is highly curable. There is low risk for recurrence or metastasis. The five-year survival rate for local melanoma, including stage one, is 98.4%. Richard will be fine.

When I tell you that the jury did not find Dr. Dealy negligent, you will not be surprised. You knew we weren't heading toward a happy ending. But I imagine you want something – some kind of revelation – to come about now.

Does it help if I tell you that one of the jurors looked as if he was going to cry, argued against letting the doctor off? He just couldn't persuade the others, couldn't turn it into *Twelve Angry Men*.

Will you be consoled if I tell you that the doctor's attorney leaned over to tell Reeny that he was sorry and that his voice broke when he apologized to her? Even he wasn't expecting the jury to decide Dr. Dealy wasn't responsible at all.

But that won't change anything.

Do you want some redemption?

Maybe you're thinking of the Scopes Monkey Trial that Reeny and I told the kids about. Maybe you're thinking of the hundred-buck fine the teacher had to pay instead of facing a jail sentence.

Nothing like that is going to happen here.

Do you want to believe that Reeny and the kids will all be alright after all?

They will and they won't.

Reeny is going to lose her job at the nursing home. She'll shout at a coworker when she goes back to work after the trial. Her boss will give her a warning at first. He'll offer her anger management classes when it happens a second time. When it happens a third time, he'll tell her he has to let her go. She and the kids will lose the house. The bank will foreclose and they will have to move in with friends.

Reeny's parents and cousins will get together and all of them will kick in to get Reeny a down payment for another house, another fixer upper. Her uncle will co-sign the loan. And eventually, Reeny will get another job – she'll work as an ambulance dispatcher.

The doctor will move to another part of the state and get another job in another clinic. And there will always be appointments available with him. And he will start driving the Humvee again.

I'm not going to end it there. I'm not going to end it with that.

This is how I am going to end it.

Reeny and I are on a train. We are fourteen years old, and we are traveling on our own, and we're going up north. We are pressing our faces to the window and we see trees, and brooks, and mountains.

And that night, for the first time in our lives, we will lift our faces to the dark sky and we will see more stars than we ever knew you could see in this world.

ACKNOWLEDGEMENTS

Lots of stuff happened while I was working on this book and there are lots of people to thank.

Once again, Influx Press inspired me to write a book I didn't know I was going to write. They did this by publishing work that defies categories, shatters classifications, and takes risks. Thank you Kit, Gary, and Sanya. And, special thanks to Kit – it was so good knowing we had the same aims as we worked on these stories together.

An Authors' Foundation Grant from the Society of Authors gave me the time and space to work on the manuscript properly. Usually when you apply for a grant you know that the odds are you won't get it. Getting this one was a surprise. The funding made a huge difference to me and so did knowing that the judges had faith in this book.

Some of these stories were first published in magazines and anthologies. 'Butterfly McQueen on Broadway' and 'The Place That He Can Never Return To' appeared in *LossLit*, 'Waiting for Daylight' appeared in the first edition of *Higher Learning: Reading and Writing About College*. 'The World's Fair' appeared on *collectedstories.com*. 'This Way to Departures' appeared in a slightly different form and with a different title in *New York Stories*. 'Missing Girl, 5, Gone Fifteen Months' appeared in the Cambridge Short Story Prize 2019 Anthology. 'Noir' first appeared as a *Kindle Single* and it was amazing to see a piece of fiction (whose length fell between story and novella) find its way out into the world digitally. Thank you, Andrew Rosenheim, for taking 'Noir' out of the slush pile and helping it find its place in the Kindle Singles store.

Rebecca Lillian and Mary Cantrell provided early feedback on 'Dangers of the Sun.' I'm grateful that they not only read through the manuscript, but didn't me when I told them the deadline. The Nuyorican and Salvadoran Spanish in 'Noir' was provided respectively by Lynley Rappaport and Francisco Javier Hernandez. Thank you both for helping my characters find a voice! Rudi Dornemann and I have been reading and critiquing each other's work for a few decades now. I have been having a blast working with him on *Why Why Why: The Books Podcast*. Speaking of which… The authors, editors, and readers who appeared on the first season of *Why Why Why* have all inspired me in some way. My thanks to all of you for talking to me about how amazing and groundbreaking British indie publishing is right now.

I first saw Copie Rodriguez's photographs of the neighhourhood where I grew up when he posted them in a Facebook group for people who grew up there. I couldn't quite believe what I was seeing at first – images of a place that seemed like a lost world to me, Washington Heights in the 1980s. I'm so grateful that one of those images became the cover of this book. If you want to see more of his work – paintings and photographs – go to www.copie157.com.

Thank you, Jamie Keenan, for designing the excellent cover.

Acknowledging the person you're closest to can be an odd thing. George already knows how grateful I am for the everything he's done to help me write this book, from listening to me talk about these stories while I've been working on them to reminding me that telling those stories is a good thing to do during the chaotic times we live in. And now, you know how grateful I am too.

Thank you, all, for helping to get this book out into the world.

ABOUT THE AUTHOR

Linda Mannheim is the author of three books of fiction: *Risk, Above Sugar Hill,* and *This Way to Departures*. Her short stories have appeared in magazines in the US, UK, South Africa, and Canada. She is currently working on *Barbed Wire Fever*, a project that explores what it means to be a refugee through writing and literature. Originally from New York, Linda divides her time between London and Berlin.

You can find out more about her work on www.lindamannheim.com.

[photo: C Leisinger]

INFLUX
PRESS

Influx Press is an independent publisher based in London, committed to publishing innovative, challenging fiction and creative non-fiction from across the UK and beyond. Formed in 2012, we have published titles ranging from award-winning fiction debuts and site-specific anthologies to squatting memoirs and radical poetry.

www.influxpress.com
@Influxpress

Lifetime supporters:
Bob West & Barbara Richards